THREE OF HEARTS

KELLY JAMIESON

Cover design by Word Sugar Designs

Formatting by Stacey Price

First edition
November, 2014

ACKNOWLEDGMENTS

I have *so* many people to thank for helping with this story!

First of all Nara Malone: you got me through such a rough place with this one—more than once!—and inspired me. I could *not* have done this story without you.

Thanks also to PG Forte and Erin Nicholas, for coming to Nashville with me, finding Haylee, Lucas, and Ben's home, visiting Broadway (although it took us two tries to actually get there), the Bluebird Café (even though we didn't get in), the Grand Ole Opry (although it was just a tour and not a concert—Nashville is crrrraaaaazy!), and for helping me pull country song lyrics out of my ass!

Super thanks to beta reader Michele Harvey who absolutely nailed the things that needed fixing in this story—but who loved it anyway. Thank you also for suggestions for fixes when I was blind to them. You helped make this book better.

Thank you also to all my amazing readers who buy and read my ménage stories . . . I hope you love Haylee, Ben, and Lucas.

And very special thanks to Sarah Frantz: thank you for inviting me to participate in this amazing charity anthology and contribute to the It Gets Better Project and be a Riptide author; thank you for the brilliant developmental editing advice you gave me; and thank you for giving me a reason to write another HEA ménage (which I love).

ABOUT THREE OF HEARTS

Haylee Tremayne is tired of the road. The concert tour for Three of Hearts was a success, but the puzzling tension between her bandmates, Ben and Lucas, is getting old. They all need some time off. Too bad it's Christmas…for Hayley, it's the most terrible time of the year.

But the day of their last concert, she discovers she's been dumped by her boyfriend for a sexy girly-girl. Story of her life—all guys ever see is tomboy Haylee. At the after-concert party, she drowns her sorrows and—desperate to feel feminine and desired for once in her life—asks Ben and Lucas for a threesome. And it's just as hot and sexy and fun as she'd hoped.

Back in Nashville, Ben and Lucas work on proving that one night wasn't a mistake, and it's amazing. But the strain between the two of them is mounting, while Haylee's own anxiety about Christmas continues to grow. The spirit of Christmas is supposed to be love, but as emotions run high and tension builds, they might be putting everything at risk...their band, their success, and worst of all...each other.

CHAPTER 1

WAITED ALL MY LIFE, WANTED SO MUCH MORE...

It should have been a good day.

It was our last night on the road before heading home to Nashville for Christmas, the last stop on our sold-out concert tour opening for country music star Clayton Walker. I wasn't looking forward to Christmas—I *hated* Christmas—but I *was* looking forward to seeing my boyfriend Doug after being away for so long touring. Doug and I had been seeing each other for about six months, and I kind of missed him. Also, my Three of Hearts bandmates Ben and Lucas weren't getting along lately. Not fighting, but I sensed a tension between them at times that bothered me. Probably they were as tired of traveling as I was. So going home was good.

But instead of having a great day, I was in my hotel room, frozen in my chair in front of my computer, staring at pictures of my boyfriend with another woman.

I'd sat down just before our concert for a quick check of email, Twitter, and Facebook, ready to message Doug something cute about seeing him tomorrow. One glance at my Facebook timeline had my lungs seizing up. I gaped at pictures of Doug with Cheyenne Ranger, a runner-up on *American Idol* a few years ago who was now super popular. And super sexy, with the whitest smile and prettiest dimples, long golden-blonde curls, and what I was pretty sure were recent breast implants.

I wasn't the most confident person about my looks, but I knew I didn't need implants.

The photographs showed Cheyenne and Doug at a club with her on his lap, their arms around each other, kissing.

As I stared at the images with horrified fascination, my stomach took a dive and my heart started sledgehammering in my chest. I couldn't help but read the editorial that went with the pictures.

"Doug," I whispered. "How could you?"

I closed my eyes and slumped back in my chair.

Well, shit.

My stomach rolled over, and I flattened my palm on my abdomen, willing away the nausea. Useless thoughts spun through my mind, like . . . maybe it wasn't what it looked like. Photographers were good at getting shots that seemed incriminating but really weren't. I'd been a victim of it myself. There was the time I'd gone out to Starbucks with no makeup and ended up on the Country Tunes website looking like a hag with big circles under my eyes. And the time I was wearing a big yellow Predators hoodie, and the photograph had made me look like I weighed two hundred pounds, and rumors started about how much weight I'd gained.

I cracked open my eyes and started scrolling and clicking around the internet. There were more photos and stories about them now being a couple. Doug being a professional hockey player and Cheyenne a rising country music star made them a popular item. There they were, smiling and gazing into each other's eyes. In another photo, he had his arm wrapped around her shoulders and his lips pressed to her temple. *Fuck.* That one really got to me because it looked so intimate . . . like he really cared about her. It must be true.

My heart constricted, and my eyes stung.

The knock at the door made me jump, but then I closed my eyes and slumped into the chair again. It was either Ben or Lucas or maybe both of them, ready to head to the concert venue.

Hobbling Christ on a crutch, I didn't want to face them, and I did *not* want to go and face the rest of the world. Jesus, there were going to be fifteen thousand people at the Tyson Events Center, and all of them would have seen my very public betrayal.

"Haylee!" Lucas called from the other side of the door. "Move your ass! We need to get out of here."

Ben and Lucas were my best friends. My family really, since my own family was fucked up and far away. I swallowed as I pushed back my chair and stumbled to the door of my room.

I turned away as Ben entered, followed by Lucas, trying to get control of my emotions. Tears had slipped out and my nose was already running. Since I was not a cute little girly girl with dimples, I was not pretty when I cried. Luckily, I didn't cry often. My life hadn't always been easy, but that had taught me the importance of always keeping a happy, smiling face in place no matter how bad things got.

"Aren't you ready?" Lucas demanded. "C'mon, Haylee."

"What're you doing, straightening your hair or something?" Ben liked to tease me about the time our manager was trying to get me to spend on my appearance.

I swiped my index finger back and forth beneath my nose. "I'm ready." My voice came out all thick. I headed back to my laptop on the desk to close it down.

"What's wrong?" Trust Ben to be the one to pick up on my mood. Although Lucas might notice something was wrong, he'd ignore it if it even hinted at some kind of display of emotion he would rather not see.

I was tempted to answer *nothing*, which would be so completely female and so completely untrue, but it also was completely not me —and the guys were going to have to know what was going on at

3

some point, because I was actually not sure if I was going to be able to perform that night. It hurt when I swallowed, but I managed to loosen my throat enough to speak. Even so, my voice shook as I gestured at the image on my laptop screen. "Check out what Doug's been doing while I've been on tour."

Lucas and Ben moved to the desk and bent their heads to study the computer.

Ben was the first to comment. "Fuck."

"Jesus Christ." Lucas leaned closer, gaping at the photo. "Who is that . . . Is that Cheyenne Ranger?"

"Yes." I twisted my fingers together and dug deep for a smile. "Don't they make a cute couple?"

Lucas's head whipped around to look at me. "Shit, Haylee, is that for real?"

I shrugged. "It appears to be. There are other pictures. They were having a nice evening at Silver Spurs last night after the game. Which she apparently was at, cheering him on."

Lucas closed his eyes briefly, but stepped toward me and wrapped me up in a hug, growling into my neck. "What an unbelievable douche bag he is."

I slid my arms around his waist and pressed my face to his chest. His hug was so warm and solid. My throat closed up again, and I squeezed my eyes shut. As I dragged in a shuddering breath through my nose, the scent of Lucas's shirt and skin filled my head, comforting and familiar—spicy masculine shower gel and the clean detergent scent of his T-shirt. His arms were strong, his chest hard beneath my cheek. Thank god I had him and Ben.

I have girlfriends back in Nashville, Georgie and Amy, but they don't get me like Ben and Lucas do. When you spend as much time together as we do—on the road, writing songs together, in the recording studio, even sharing a house—you get to know one another pretty well, and Lucas and Ben probably knew the real me better than anyone in the world.

Lucas stroked my hair. "Asshole," he muttered. "I'm gonna kick his ass next time I see him." This was his version of sympathy: a hug and a threat to kick Doug's ass.

I couldn't help the smile that tugged my lips. "He's six foot four, two hundred thirty pounds." Lucas knew this, but I figured it wouldn't hurt to remind him. "He beats people up for a living."

That wasn't true; Doug was a tough player but not a goon. But I *had* seen him fight a couple of times, which had alarmed me to no end, and he was definitely good at it.

"True. But I can take him."

I lifted my head to look up at him. His scowl was ferocious, and Doug might have a few inches and pounds on him, but Lucas was tall and built too. But I'd still be worried Lucas would get pounded. "No you can't."

"Hey!" He directed his displeasure at me, but his eyes were soft. "I'm offended by your lack of confidence in my fighting skills."

I gave him a shaky smile and drew back from him. "Thank you," I whispered.

Ben was right behind me. "You okay, Haylee?"

I turned to face him. His eyebrows sloped downward and the corners of his mouth were tight. I could tell he was feeling my pain. Ben was more sensitive and emotional than Lucas. His reaction wouldn't be to punch Doug—which was a good thing, given that he was just under six feet tall, and leaner than Lucas—but I could see his concern.

"Not really." My lips trembled. "It's all over the internet! How am I supposed to get up on stage tonight in front of all those people after being humiliated like that?"

They each gave me a bleak look. I loved them, but hey, they weren't always the best at dealing with tears and emotional females. Ben was better at it than Lucas, but his moods vacillated more and sometimes he ended up all broody too. I'm not usually a temperamental female, but in all honesty, I get wicked PMS about every third month and they still get fidgety about it. Not that I had PMS just then. But getting dumped so publicly and so . . . treacherously was enough to make even me tear up. It really did hurt.

Lucas finally came up with, "You can do it." He pulled me in for another hug.

"This sucks, Haylee," Ben said in his quiet way. "He's a dick-head. Forget about him. He's not worth it. We got your back, sweetheart."

My heart expanded hard against my breastbone at their staunch support. I moved away from Lucas, dropped back into the chair at the desk, and slumped down. Ben and Lucas exchanged concerned glances.

"Haylee. You gotta get your shit together for the concert." Lucas's golden eyebrows drew together. I knew he was concerned, but as always, he was also focused on the goal.

"I know. I will. I'm fine."

"Did you really care that much about him?" Ben leaned on the desk near me.

"Well, sure." I thought about that for a second. "Of course I did. He's . . . I mean, I *thought* he was a great guy." I made a face, then sighed. "It figures he'd go for someone like Cheyenne."

Once again I caught their exchange of eye contact. "Why's that, babe?" Lucas asked.

My head jerked back a little at such a stupid question. "Because she's gorgeous," I said. "Blonde and pretty and sexy."

"So are you." This from Ben.

I snorted. "Riiiight." It was sweet of him to say, though.

"You're blonde," Lucas pointed out. My eyebrows flew up, and he realized how that had sounded. "And pretty and sexy," he added hastily. Then he muttered, "Fuck."

"No, I'm not." They both opened their mouths, and I held up a hand. "Don't even say it. You know I'm not. And the only reason I'm blonde is thanks to Salon Giorgio." My hair had been blonde when I was a little girl, especially in summers when I practically lived outside, but over the years it had darkened to mousy brown. Our manager, Brandon, had sent me to Salon Giorgio earlier in the year for a makeover, and now every six to eight weeks I had to endure a couple of hours in a chair looking like a space alien with my hair all wrapped up in tin foil. "Cheyenne Ranger probably looks like that every day of her life." I threw my hand out toward the picture on my computer screen. "Even when she gets out of bed in the morning." And then thinking about her getting out of bed with Doug made my heart hurt again.

Ben snorted. "Okay, she's cute and sexy, but come on. It takes major effort to look like that."

"Not to mention surgery," Lucas added, no doubt alluding to the suspected implants.

I grinned. "I love you guys."

"Look." Ben dropped to a crouch in front of me and grabbed my hands. "You're gorgeous and talented. Doug's a dumb fuck. We need you on that stage tonight focused on the music. Are you gonna be able to do that?"

I pressed my lips together. "Of course I can." I wasn't as confident as my words sounded but there was no way in hell I'd let the guys down.

"You're a professional," Lucas added. "You'll be fine."

I nodded. I *was* a professional. But my chest was aching, my stomach was churning, and my throat was tightening up again; only a whisper came out when I spoke. "Shit. That asswipe."

"Channel it into your music." Ben's eyes met mine. "You can put all that emotion into the songs. It's a great way to let it out."

I smiled and squeezed his hands. "Thanks. I'll try." I lifted my chin and straightened my shoulders, then snapped the lid of my laptop down forcefully as if shutting Doug Brandt out of my life.

It was good advice. Because as we say in the biz, the show must go on.

CHAPTER 2
I SHOULDN'T WANT THESE THINGS,
ESPECIALLY FROM YOU . . .

I took Ben's advice and put everything I had into our music. The disappointment and humiliation and even anger all came out. These were emotions I'd experienced before. I had to fight the rush of memories these feelings brought back: memories of that horrendous Christmas when I'd been seventeen and feeling like this on stage. Only this time I wasn't alone, like I'd felt back then. Now I had Lucas and Ben.

Lucas and I sang to each other on stage with a passion and intensity I don't think we'd ever had, and the crowd loved it. When we sang "All of You," staring into each other's eyes, full of angst and yearning, the audience hushed and then exploded. I needed a moment after that song, and Lucas had to improvise with the crowd as I composed myself.

I wanted to kill out there. The short, skintight, gold-sequined dress was the sexiest one I owned. I'd let the makeup artist polish my arms and legs, and I was wearing gold satin platform pumps with five-inch heels. I owned those shoes and how powerful they made me feel, strutting and planting my feet as I sang into the mike. I shook my hair back, let my entire body get into the music, and laid it all down there on the stage.

I knew it was ridiculous—that Doug wasn't there and would never see the concert—but I wanted to show him what he was missing. And somehow, because of those old memories, I was also showing my dad who I'd become.

I love performing. Seriously, all that attention on me just makes me come alive. Most of the time, I'm energized by it. It's what I live for: entertaining, pleasing a crowd, singing. But tonight, by the time we'd finished our second encore and left the stage, I was exhausted and filled with a whole storm of emotions I had a hard time sorting out. All I wanted to do was go back to my hotel room and curl into the fetal position in my bed for about a year.

But somehow Lucas and Ben pushed me along once we returned to the hotel, and there we were at the after-party in Clayton's suite. It was packed with people—some music biz people, our agent, our manager, our producer, Clayton's people, and a whole lot of groupie girls. Jason Aldean's "My Kinda Party" played loudly enough that hotel security had probably needed a bribe to ignore it.

Lucas and Ben filled plates from the extravagant buffet set up in the suite, handed me one, and proceeded to devour meatballs, shrimp, and smoked salmon. I picked at a few things, not really hungry, but guzzled down glass after glass of champagne. Beer was usually my drink of choice, but the champagne tasted pretty damn good and was giving me a pleasant buzz.

I became aware that the music playing in the background had changed to Rascal Flatts's "I'll Be Home for Christmas." *Blergh*. My skin crawled and my stomach twisted into knots at the familiar yet dreaded Christmas song. Now I really didn't feel like eating.

"Are you gonna eat that?" Ben pointed at an untouched skewer of chicken on my plate.

"Nah." I offered him the plate.

"Shut the fuck up." Lucas elbowed in between us to snag the skewer. "I want it."

"You just ate ten of those!" Ben tried to grab it back. "And there are more on the table."

"Suck my dick." Lucas gave him the look, the one he was so good at: one corner of his mouth lifted and the opposite eyebrow raised. It was super sexy and wicked, and he was famous for it.

"In your dreams," Ben said.

"Yeah right. As if I'm that desperate."

Which was undoubtedly true. Both guys had girls following them around constantly. Groupies lined up at the front of the stage, trying to get their attention. In fact, there were lots here at the party giving them the eye. I sighed. "I'll go get you more."

"No." Ben stopped me. "Lucas is just being an asshole."

This banter went on all the time between Lucas and Ben. And me, when I was on my game. But tonight, I'd noticed an edge to it.

"I need another drink." I moved to the bar that had been set up on a table. The suite was luxurious—well, as luxurious as you could get in Sioux City, Iowa. Far nicer than my room, anyway. I surveyed the selections. I was feeling the effects of all the champagne, and another glass probably wouldn't be smart. Another drink *period* probably wasn't smart, but I was also not in a mood to be smart. I was exhausted and sad and kinda . . . pissy.

I went for a beer. My feet were killing me in my heels, so I turned and tried not to limp as I carried my beer over to a couch. I sat, tugging my short dress down on my thighs, now not so comfortable showing that much. On stage I was finally learning not to constantly do that—it just drew attention to my awkwardness in such girly clothing. But now, I couldn't stop myself from adjusting the drapey neckline, checking my cleavage, and pulling on the hem.

I grew up in Grand Forks, North Dakota, a tomboy who played baseball and basketball, loved fishing and ATVing. I'd read the press about my lack of style. My voice has been described as raw and sexy, but on stage, my jeans and baggy shirts and boots were decid-edly *un*sexy. Brandon had been working with me to try to glam up my image, and I hated it and all the memories it brought back from when I was a kid. I felt like a fraud in short, sparkly dresses, and at first I'd teetered dangerously around the stage on platform heels. But I did it for my bandmates Lucas and Ben because I loved them and we all wanted to succeed at this.

I stretched my legs out straight to admire the shoes. Damn. My legs did look pretty good, the shine on them making them appear way more feminine than I'd always thought they were with the muscles I had from playing baseball and basketball.

Brandon sat beside me. "Hey, Haylee. Great concert."

"Thanks."

He started going on about the crowd reaction, especially to "All of You" and one of our new songs, "Treasure." I hadn't said anything to him about Doug, and I guessed he didn't know or didn't care—and why would he? I mean, I knew he cared about us, but for him, this was all business.

I watched Lucas across the room, now talking to two girls—one with long, curly dark hair hanging down her back, the other with perfectly straight auburn hair, both slender and glamorous in tight jeans, stiletto heels, and skimpy tops. The groupies had made their move.

My gaze wandered around, searching for Ben, and found him in a similar situation, only with just one girl, a Heidi Klum look-alike. A guy had once told me I reminded him of Heidi Klum, and I'd laughed so hard I'd pulled a muscle. Ben was listening to Heidi talk, but when I followed his gaze across the room . . . he was watching Lucas. Huh.

As always, they were the center of female attention at any gath-ering, and I was sitting alone on the couch with Brandon, who was probably going to tell me that I needed to get my eyebrows waxed or collagen injections in my lips.

KELLY JAMIESON

"I need another drink," I stated when I could get a word in. I gave him a bright smile as I rose to my feet. "Will you excuse me?"

Of course he agreed, and I made my way back to the bar. I grabbed another beer from a silver tub of ice, cracked it open, and drank straight from the bottle. Crisp and cold, the liquid bubbled down my throat. I resisted the urge to swipe the back of my hand across my mouth when I lowered the bottle. But as I turned, I caught Ben's eye. He was watching me, lips quirked.

I gave him a crooked smile and lifted my bottle in a wry toast. Perhaps my guzzling half the bottle at once amused him. I'd impressed the guys early into our acquaintanceship with my beer-chugging skills—learned, I'm sad to say, in high school.

Ben grinned and turned back to the tall blonde, who'd set her hand on his arm and said something to him.

I wandered up to our drummer, Tim, who was talking to some of Clayton's back-up band, and they easily shifted to include me in the conversation. I didn't feel like talking, but they were having a good laugh about a screw up that happened during Clayton's concert, that he'd handled like the experienced professional he was.

Some movement near the door caught my attention, and I looked over to see Lucas and the two girls leaving together.

I pursed my lips and suppressed a sigh. He was such a dawg. This wouldn't be his first threesome. I also knew he and Ben had had threesomes together where they'd shared a girl, and, one memorable night I'd accidentally stumbled upon them in a four-some with two girls.

Neither of them had had a long-term relationship in the two years I'd known them. I suspected Ben was wary because of having had his heart broken by someone, though he'd never been forth-coming with details. Lucas just laughed when I asked him why he didn't have a girlfriend, making some smartass comment about how no woman would put up with him for long.

It didn't normally disturb me that they did kinky things like three-ways, but I guess because tonight I was teetering on the edge of depression, it kind of bummed me a bit. Knowing I'd go back to my room alone didn't usually bother me because I'd think about going home to Doug, but now Doug was an asshole and I was alone.

I stared glumly down at my gold shoes.

I should just leave.

As I turned to walk out, the room spun just a teeny bit around me. Whoa. Apparently the champagne and the beers were now entering my bloodstream. Well, good. Maybe I should have one more before I left, and then I could just stumble in my high-heeled shoes and sparkly dress down to my room three floors below and pass out on my bed. I headed back toward the bar, but before I got there Ben stepped in front of me.

"Hey hon." He narrowed his eyes a bit. "Think you've had enough?"

"Probably," I said agreeably, pushing past him to get to the beer.

He took hold of my arm, and his hand was big and strong on my bare biceps. "You okay?"

I pulled out a smile. "Of course."

"Then why're you drinking like a frat boy on Friday night?"

I had to laugh. "Because that's my roots, Benny."

His lips twitched at the nickname. I was the only one who ever called him that, and he hated it. Which is pretty much why I did it. Pushing his buttons amused me.

"I know," he said. "You ready to go?"

"I was going to have one more beer."

"Honey, you're about two chugs away from passed out on the floor."

I sighed. He wasn't wrong.

"Let's go now." He steered me away from the bar and toward the door. I tried to dig my stiletto heels in, but he was way bigger and stronger than me. "C'mon."

Whatever. I'd been ready to leave anyway and didn't want to

make a big scene. It was the last night of a successful tour, everyone was happy, and I sure didn't want to blow another opportunity to go on the road with someone like Clayton Walker.

Ben glanced back to the suite as we stepped into the hall. "Where's Lucas?"

"He left a few minutes ago with two hot chicks."

His mouth tightened, and his eyebrows lowered.

I held my hand out to the wall, trailing my fingers along it for balance as we walked. "D'you wish you were with them?" I couldn't help but ask.

"Jesus, Haylee." He pulled his cell phone out as we walked—he walked, I staggered—down the plush carpet of the hall. He let go of me long enough to thumb in a text message and then we were standing—he stood, I wavered—in front of the elevator.

After he pressed the down button, I leaned against him, laying my head on his chest, and sighed. "Oh Benny . . . I love you."

His body tensed, so briefly I might have imagined it, and then he kissed the top of my head. "Love you too, hon. Let's get you down to your room."

The elevator doors slid open, and we stepped in. Once in the elevator, I slid my arms around his waist and snuggled into him. He felt so good, big and warm and strong, and he smelled good too; his arms coming around me comforted me. "I'm sorry," I mumbled to his chest. "Maybe I did drink a little too much."

"I've seen you worse."

Yeah, he had. I twisted my mouth up at that, preferring not to be reminded that he'd seen me at my worshipping-the-porcelain-altar worst.

Don't think I'm a lush or an alcoholic or anything. I grew up with an alcoholic father and hated it. I also know I don't have that kind of relationship with booze. But there'd been a few nights of hard partying with the guys since we'd gotten together. It kind of went with the territory, and I was determined that no guy would drink me under the table. In the two years we'd been together, I'd been puking drunk once. But Ben had seen it.

And amazingly, he still loved me.

As a friend. That's what all that love talk meant. We were friends. Partners. Him and Lucas and me.

And I was having a bad night, that was all.

The elevator door opened. Ben guided me out into the hall, and I blinked to see Lucas leaning against the wall outside my room, arms crossed.

"How'd you get here?" I frowned at him. "I thought you were off somewhere having a threesome."

He straightened. "Not tonight. Where's your key?"

I dug in my purse and found it; Lucas plucked it from my fingers and pushed it into the slot. I laughed.

They both looked at me.

"What?" I walked past them into my room. I tried to strut, but my feet were seriously killing me in those fucking heels.

Ben closed the door behind us. "What's so funny?"

Lucas flicked on a lamp, and I threw myself into a chair and lifted a foot to take off the strappy platform shoes. "You pushed the key into the slot," I mumbled. Okay, maybe it wasn't as dirty as it had sounded in my head.

"Here hon, let me help you." Ben went to his knees on the carpet in front of me, and something inside me went all warm and soft as he held my foot and unbuckled the tiny strap. I just stared at him as he concentrated, setting the shoe aside, lowering my foot, and picking up the other one. And his fingers on my ankle suddenly made me tingle.

His fingertips were rough from playing guitar and fiddle. The gentle abrasion made all my nerve endings quiver. Then he held my foot, my heel in his palm, his other hand stroking over my instep, and a shudder worked its way over my entire body.

"Feet hurt?" he murmured.

I could only nod, my mouth suddenly dry. I complained vociferously about wearing high-heeled shoes, which was why he'd asked. But I no longer felt any pain from my feet, only heat and . . . tremors.

Ben stood and moved away, and I set my bare feet on the soft carpet, blinking. I clutched the armrests of the chair.

Lucas had turned on the TV and settled onto the bed with pillows tucked behind him. I turned my attention to him. "What are you doing?"

"Just seeing what's on TV."

I pursed my lips. "You guys don't have to stay with me. I'm fine."

They both lifted their big shoulders, Ben taking a seat in another chair, watching the TV too. "We can stay for a while," he said. "Wanna make sure you're okay."

"I said I'm fine." I stood, proud of my perfect balance now that I no longer had to deal with spindly heels.

"Sure, babe."

I gave a small huff and set my hands on my hips.

"Give me the remote," Ben ordered Lucas.

"Like hell." Lucas kept it firmly in his hand, surfing through the available channels.

Ben frowned and crossed his arms. "For fuck's sake. How can you find something to watch when you go that fast?"

Lucas gave Ben a brief narrow-eyed look, then ignored him.

I bit my lip. There was that edge again. This wasn't the first time they'd argued over the remote or what to watch, but tonight it felt . . . tense.

Whatever. They wanted to stay and watch TV and argue over the remote, fine. I rolled my eyes and headed to the bathroom. I stood in front of the wall of mirrors, hands on the edge of the marble counter, and lifted my chin. I wasn't really that drunk.

Maybe it wasn't something to be proud of, but I could hold my liquor.

My face still looked unfamiliar with all the makeup I had to wear for performances. At first, I'd felt like I had a mask on all the time. Now I was getting used to the feel of it. I tipped my head. My flat-ironed, highlighted hair fell forward over my shoulder. I saw flawless skin, smoky eyes, shiny lips.

I closed my eyes, assailed by a fresh wash of sadness at Doug's perfidy.

I'd never been exactly sure what Doug Brandt had seen in me. He was a professional hockey player with the Nashville Predators— a talented athlete, a multimillionaire, good-looking (yes, he had all his own teeth) with a killer body. Whereas I was . . . nobody.

Well, not exactly nobody. Three of Hearts was doing well. Last year we'd released our debut album, and our lead-off single "All of You" had peaked at number two on *Billboard*'s Hot Country Songs. We'd won a Grammy for Best New Artist and were nominated for a few CMT Music Awards. Just before this tour we'd released our second album *Pictures on Silence* and the concert tour had been sold out in every city. So I wasn't *nobody*, but I didn't know if the day would ever come when I'd feel like . . . somebody.

I kept thinking about Cheyenne, how perfect and beautiful she was. No wonder Doug had dumped me. He wasn't the first guy this had happened with. Guys always saw me as one of them—a sister, a buddy. Chugging beer and playing basketball and belching out loud. I'd always had lots of guy friends, and they liked me, but they stared at and drooled over the other girls, the ones in skirts and makeup and curls, like the girls who'd been up in Clayton's suite, all easy in their glam gorgeousness.

I walked back out of the bathroom. Lucas and Ben were both on the bed: Lucas now on his stomach, head at the foot of the bed, and Ben reclining on the pillows.

The bed was king-size, but two big men took up a lot of room. I stood there, hands on my hips, eyebrows raised. "What are you watching?"

They looked up at me and for a moment I felt . . . studied. Their gazes tracked up and down my body, from my bare feet and legs to my tight dress and back down. My immediate response was to snap something like, "Take a picture, it'll last longer" or "Put your eyes back in your damn heads, it's me, for god's sake." But for some reason, the words didn't come out, and I felt a tingly sensation all through my body. Appallingly, my nipples tingled most of all, contracting into hard points. Oops. I didn't have a bra on, and I wasn't sure if they could see my nipples through the sequined dress.

They'd seen me dressed like this a hundred times. A thousand. Whatever.

"*Walk the Line*. Come watch with us." Ben patted the mattress beside him, between him and Lucas. Johnny Cash. I loved that movie. I crawled up between them.

But I wasn't comfortable. The short skirt rode high on my thighs. I tried to ignore it, but they kept glancing at my legs. At me. My nerves twitched. The air thickened. Awareness vibrated around me.

My forehead tightened as I tried to focus on the television, tried to relax in my bed.

Ben slouched lower on the pillows and slipped his arm behind my shoulders. "Don't be sad. That asshole isn't worth it."

"I'm okay." My voice came out small.

Ben gave a soft laugh and hugged me tighter. "That's what you always say."

"But I always am okay. Right?" I tipped my head to look up at him.

"Yeah. You always are, sweetheart."

"I just . . ." I couldn't even go there, and say what I was so afraid of.

"What, babe?" Lucas muted the TV, rolled to his side, and turned to face us, elbow on the mattress, hand supporting his head.

I lowered my gaze to my hands clasped on my stomach and expelled a hard breath. "Nothing." I narrowed my gaze at Lucas. "Why aren't you with those girls?"

I sensed Ben's body tensing at my question.

Lucas shrugged. "Not tonight."

"Did Ben ask you to come here?"

Lucas smiled. "Yeah."

"You didn't have to do that."

"You're hurting. Of course I'm here for you. Not gonna leave you alone at a time like this."

My chest ached. "Thank you," I whispered. Trust Ben to be the one who took care of me. Not that Lucas didn't. He just wasn't as sensitive as Ben. He could come across as unemotional, but I knew Lucas did have feelings under that take-charge exterior. Unfamiliar tears once again prickled at the corners of my eyes, and I squeezed them shut briefly. "You know what? I don't really care that much about Doug. I just feel like such a big loser."

Ben gasped. "You are not a loser."

"Shut the fuck up." Lucas pushed up to sitting. Again, his way of comforting me didn't exactly ooze tenderness. But I knew without a doubt he was sincere.

"Haylee." Ben tipped my chin up so our eyes met. "Tonight on that stage—you were fucking on fire, you were so hot."

I blinked at him.

"Didn't you feel it?" Lucas asked. "You were so into the music. Putting everything you had into it . . ."

"It's true." Ben shifted closer as he affirmed what Lucas had said. "I could feel it. There wasn't a person in the audience who could take their eyes off you." He hesitated, the corners of his eyes tightening ever so slightly, his mouth lifting at one corner. "You two looked smokin' hot together."

He was in a better position to judge, being our back-up vocalist. I'd been so swept up in the emotion, I'd barely been aware there were people watching until the applause had exploded.

Ben lifted some hair away from my face and tucked it behind my ear. "You're gorgeous. Mesmerizing. Sexy as fucking hell. It wasn't only the audience who couldn't take their eyes off you."

I stared into Ben's eyes, and something shifted in them and inside me.

CHAPTER 3
I'VE NEVER FELT THIS WAY BEFORE

Your touch, your smile, your arms around me . . .

My heart started beating faster and once again my skin tingled everywhere. The way Ben was looking at me was different, his eyes warm and intent.

I became acutely aware that we were all in a bed together. Well, *on* the bed, but still, we were all very close together, close enough that I could smell their unique fragrances, close enough to feel their body heat, close enough to touch. Lucas, Ben, and I practically lived together on the road, spending hours in that damn tour bus, and we *literally* lived together back in Nashville—as in, we shared a house. But we'd never all been on a bed together like this, with Ben gazing at me as if he wanted . . . something.

I blinked and turned my head on the pillow to peer at Lucas, who was watching Ben and me with a notch between his eyebrows. He looked from Ben to me, then back to Ben with narrowed eyes.

"He's right." Lucas leaned in closer, meeting my eyes. "I got hard when we were singing 'All of You.' When you slid your hand around the back of my neck and put your forehead against mine . . . Fuck, that was hot."

Whoa. That was . . . bold of Lucas to tell me that.

When I'd leaned into him like that, he'd wrapped an arm around my waist and pulled me up against him, and we'd moved together to the music in a slow, sensual dance, body to body. "Th-that was just part of the act." Hearing about Lucas's hard-on made my insides start to shiver.

He grimaced. "Yeah. I know. You're all brokenhearted about some other guy. It wasn't like you were really coming on to me."

My mouth fell open. Did he *want* me to come on to him?

"I don't think I'm really all that brokenhearted." I sighed. "Rejection sucks, though."

He slowly nodded. Ben's hand cupped my shoulder, then began stroking up and down my upper arm. I glanced back at him. He gave me a nod. "Yeah. It does. But Haylee . . ."

I licked my lips, and when his gaze dropped to my mouth, my stomach did a slow, lovely roll. My eyes widened, then moved to his mouth. Which was a very attractive mouth.

This wasn't news to me. I always knew how beautiful these guys were. Ben's darker skin and hair contrasted Lucas's tawny coloring. Lucas's hair was longer and all messy on top. His nose was a bit broad and unevenly shaped, and when he smiled, deep dimples made girls go all silly. Lucas wore a heavy stubble of light-brown whiskers, Ben a short, dark beard.

I was thinking about kissing Ben's beautiful mouth.

This should have been shocking. Maybe the alcohol made it less so. Or maybe I had to admit it wasn't actually the first time I'd ever thought about kissing Ben. But since we'd joined up to form Three of Hearts, it had been a business relationship that had turned to friendship, and never anything more. The guys had had tons of girls, though nothing lasting, and more than their share of hookups and dates. My own love life hadn't been so interesting until Doug had come along. Bleh.

"What?" I whispered at Ben's unfinished sentence.

His mouth went solemn. "I kinda hate to say it, but I'm glad you're not with him anymore."

My eyebrows lifted. "I thought you liked him. I mean, up until today."

He hitched one big shoulder. "Not so much."

"Oh."

"Me neither," Lucas stated firmly. "Never liked him."

Well. I wasn't sure what to do with that. But I guess it didn't really matter whether they liked Doug or not, since we were done.

I studied Ben's lean, oblong face with its narrow, sculpted jaw. Sideburns tapered down into his dark beard, and thick eyelashes gave his blue eyes a very intense appearance. His T-shirt had ridden up on his abdomen, revealing a strip of tanned skin and a narrow trail of dark hair that led down into his low-rise Levis.

I swallowed. Once again, I should have been shocked that my eyes followed that trail of hair and went even lower, to the definite bulge behind the buttons. But once again, I had to admit that I'd looked there before.

In complete innocence, of course.

Heat washed down through my body. Ben continued to stroke my arm and my skin was super sensitized. An ache developed low in my belly. The air around us went electric.

Lucas lifted a hand and touched my face, so gently. His thumb brushed over my bottom lip. "Don't understand why you think you're not attractive, Haylee. Look at you." His gaze dropped to my mouth, then to my breasts.

More heat suffused me. My breasts swelled and my nipples tightened, and I closed my eyes, filled with a hungry yearning. My breath came in short, shallow bursts. What was happening here? Lucas and Ben were regarding me as if they wanted to eat me up, and that was

23

. . . exciting. No. I mean, that was wrong. We didn't have that kind of relationship.

"What's it like to have a threesome?" I asked.

Oh. My. God. Did I really just say that? My face flamed.

Ben and Lucas looked at each other over me. One corner of Lucas's mouth kicked up into that smile, and Ben's mouth did a slow curve. Something passed between them, some unspoken message and agreement. I sank my teeth into my bottom lip.

Ben turned his hot gaze back on me. The air sizzled around us. "Wanna find out?"

My head spun. It wasn't the alcohol. Definitely not. It was a dizzying burst of lust, along with a warm slide of desire pooling between my thighs.

I did want to find out. I really, really did. The focused attention of two guys on me, all on me, was so fucking hot. I'd never had that before, and in my current visit to Loserville it was so tempting, so . . . irresistible.

At that moment, *I* felt irresistible. Sexy. Ready to abandon myself to it, to abnegate all rational, sensible thought, to just feel and be sensual and carnal and enjoy the experience. I'd had brief glimpses of this kind of feeling in my life, but not enough. Never enough.

I closed my eyes briefly. The urge came over me, and I shouldn't have done it, but somehow I couldn't stop myself. I sat up and reached for the side zip of my dress. I drew it down and the snug garment loosened, the straps sliding down my arms and the bodice falling to my waist.

If the air around us had been electrified before, now it was snapping with sparks. Both guys drew in a sharp breath. For a few painful seconds, I hoped like hell I hadn't misread their signals. If they rejected me now, I would die. I would bury myself under the duvet and never, ever come out. Okay, I'd come out, but when I did, I'd be on the next flight to Alaska.

"Jesus fuck," Lucas breathed.

"Holy hell," Ben said.

"Yes, I want to find out," I whispered.

My heart pounded against my ribs, and then Ben leaned up and put his lips on my shoulder. He stayed like that for a long moment as Lucas sat back up. I met Lucas's eyes and the smoldering heat in them had my breath stalling in my throat.

"Serious?" He held my gaze.

I nodded.

"You sure, babe?"

"I'm sure." I was so *not* sure, but backing down now would be embarrassing. And I wanted to know what it felt like to be desired, to be the focus of two hot guys. I wanted that enough to push my doubts and worries aside and go for it.

Ben and Lucas exchanged another look and then they both moved in on me. Ben reached for my waist, while Lucas cupped my jaw in his callused hand and leaned in for a kiss.

My lips parted and clung to his, and I melted.

His mouth moved on mine, firm and warm, brushing my lips once, twice, then drawing back. His eyes met mine again. That eyebrow lifted and the opposite corner of his mouth kicked up. "Nice," he said, his eyelids drooping, and he kissed me again. This time his mouth was harder, more demanding. His thumb exerted gentle pressure on my chin, encouraging my mouth to open too. I didn't need much encouragement as my body softened. My mouth felt hungry for the taste of him, and our tongues slid together. Heat flowed through my veins and a knot of ache developed between my legs.

Ben's hands held my waist from behind, and Lucas drew back. We stared at each other.

"Holy shit balls," I breathed, my heart tapping out a rapid beat. I saw the same sentiment in Lucas's wide eyes and parted lips, his rapid breathing.

"Fuck." Ben lifted me up, shifting us both so I sat between his spread thighs, my back to his chest. He swept my hair aside and put his mouth on the side of my neck. Shivers cascaded over my body, along with tingling warmth. One of his hands slid around my ribcage, just below my breast, and the other curved around my neck, his fingertips brushing my throat, sliding up to my chin, and then he eased my head back to his shoulder so he, too, could find my mouth.

My mind disintegrated while my body dissolved in sensation. Thoughts fragmented, heat washed down through me as Ben's tongue caressed mine, his fingers tightening on my ribs, my breasts swelling. One of my hands came up to cover his and my toes curled into the silky duvet.

Ben's mouth clung to mine. He tasted different from Lucas, and his lips felt thinner, but they were both very good kissers. Better than good. Stupendously good. Then he lifted his mouth from mine and strung kisses along my jaw, over to just below my ear. Shivers spread over my skin and a moan swelled in my throat. He opened his mouth on the sensitive skin at the side of my neck and gently sucked.

I gasped as he cupped my bare breasts. That felt so good. A groan rumbled from his chest—which I took to mean that it felt good for him too—and my pussy tightened.

My eyes fluttered open although my head felt too heavy to lift from Ben's shoulder. Lucas was in front of me, watching us with hot eyes. He tugged on my dress, which was crumpled at my waist, and helped me lift my ass off the mattress briefly so he could pull the dress down over my legs. He tossed it into a sparkly heap on the carpet, then gently parted my legs and knelt between them. His gaze roamed from Ben's hands on my breasts, up to my face, then back down to my boy short panties, sitting low on my hipbones.

"Haylee," he said, voice husky. "How could you possibly think you're not sexy? Look at you."

I blinked, and Ben's hands gently squeezed my full breasts. My nipples throbbed against his palms. "God that feels good," I gasped.

"Your tits are amazing," Ben rasped beside my ear. He nuzzled my hair. "Fucking amazing." And then his thumbs brushed down over my nipples. A hard shudder worked over my entire body. I arched my back into his touch. "So sensitive." He stroked his thumbs back and forth over the tender tips, and a sweet ache blossomed there and spread down to my pussy.

"This is crazy," I managed to articulate, although the words slurred.

Ben filled his hands with my breasts again. "D'you want to stop?"

I panted and moved my head in the negative. "Please no, god, no."

Lucas spanned my waist with his hands. Now four hands were touching my body. It was shocking and carnal and sublime. He bent forward and put his mouth on my belly, and the muscles there jumped at his touch. He paused, eyes closed, and breathed in. "You smell so damn good, Haylee."

Oh dear Lord. That just made me melt even more, and my legs shifted on the bed. Lucas kissed my hipbones, laying a trail of kisses across my tummy between them, then hooked his thumbs into the top edge of my boy shorts. He looked up at me.

My eyelids felt heavy, my body filled with warm languor. Our eyes met though, and I read the question.

The sweetness of their willingness to continue to check in with me and confirm my participation only seduced me more. Somewhere in the back of my head I knew this was probably a bad idea, but I was drunk—no longer on alcohol, but on sensation—and I felt safe with them. My two best friends, men I knew cared about me. Although not like this. Never like this.

I wanted this. I wanted more.

"Do it," I whispered.

Lucas held my gaze steadily as he began to tug my panties down over my hips. I lifted my butt, pushing back into Ben's big hard body while he toyed with my nipples. He caught them between his thumbs and forefingers in gentle, rhythmic pinches, sending streamers of hot liquid pleasure right to my core.

Right to where Lucas was now staring as he slowly dragged my shorts down over my thighs. I bent my knees up toward my chest and he whisked the underwear over my feet and tossed them aside. Suddenly a little modest, I lowered my feet to the mattress, keeping my knees together. He circled my ankles with his fingers, so gently. His rough fingertips caressed the sensitive skin behind each ankle bone, but he took his time, a faint smile touching his lips. Anticipation sizzled under my skin, that hot ache between my legs intensifying.

Ben's mouth on my neck, my ear, my hair, his hands on my breasts tugging my nipples into stiff, aching points, and Lucas's caresses on my ankles stirred my senses up into something raw and tender and deliciously expectant. My mouth opened with a hunger that echoed the ache in my pussy, but still Lucas moved with tantalizing slowness, running his hands up and down my calves. When his fingertips brushed the backs of my knees, I jolted. When he lifted my feet higher and brought them to his mouth to kiss the insteps, first one, them the other, his gaze fixed on mine the entire time, I shuddered.

"Christ, you're so responsive," Ben muttered in my ear. He licked the side of my neck. "Feel good, sweetheart?"

My mouth had gone dry and the word came out choked. "Y-yes." I swallowed and wet my lips, making Lucas's eyes flare. "So good."

He continued to caress my calves, then his hands slid up past my knees and once more parted my thighs. Heat washed down over me from my hairline to my toes as he exposed my sex to his gaze. His mouth went full and soft as he looked at me.

I thought I might die of the fire that licked along every nerve ending on my body. Our chorus of labored breathing filled the room, the only light the television flickering mutely. None of us said a word. Ben's breathing was loudest in my ear, his hands squeezing my breasts with erotic pressure. Lucas closed his eyes briefly, almost reverently.

I read the signs of their arousal, and it thrilled me to my core. I dragged my tongue across my lips again, my breasts lifting in Ben's hands as I fought to breathe. Then Ben broke the silence with a raspy, "Lick her pussy."

Lucas's gaze flicked up to Ben. The corner of his mouth lifted, then his eyes met mine again. I struggled to focus on him, my body quivering so hard. "You want that, Haylee? Want me to lick your pussy?"

Helpless, hypnotized, I nodded.

"It's so pretty," Lucas said, and I didn't know if he was telling Ben or giving me a compliment. Or maybe both. He leaned closer. More heat shimmered beneath my skin. I'd never been studied so intently, so intimately. I'd never watched a man's eyes glitter and his cheeks flush as he stared at me there, and my stomach did a flip of excitement that I was getting that reaction from him. Me.

My teeth sank into my bottom lip, and my hips lifted off the bed.

"Oh yeah," Lucas said on a small laugh. "Greedy little pussy. You want it bad, don't you?"

I couldn't stop the noise that escaped my throat, a sound I'd never made before, something raw and dirty and pleading.

I loved dirty talk in bed. Some guys are good at it, some just sound gross, and others don't say a word. Lucas was good at it. As in, *good*.

"Look at you. Pink and swollen. Shiny wet." Blunt, callused fingertips brushed over my lips there. The ache behind my clit deepened and my ass squeezed with the urge to lift myself up to him, so

29

shamelessly needy. "Your clit's hard." He circled it with one fingertip.

More heat blazed through my body. I whimpered.

"Christ, I want to taste you," he murmured, his attention still focused there raptly. "Wanna see if you taste as good as I think. As good as you smell."

"I was sweating up on stage a few hours ago. I'm probably not, um, very fresh."

He laughed. "You smell fucking fantastic." He pressed his cheek to my inner thigh, lightly abrading the tender skin there with his beard stubble. He turned his face and opened his mouth slowly on my thigh, and I watched his tongue come out and lick me as he laid kisses up toward my center.

My breathing suspended, my lungs burned, and my body trembled with the anticipation of his mouth on me.

CHAPTER 4

WAITED ALL MY LIFE, WANTED SO MUCH MORE

"Oh yeah." Ben's voice rumbled in my ear. "Fuck yeah, lick her pussy. And then it's my turn."

Lucas gave Ben a gleaming-eyed look, then kissed me between my legs, the same long, slow, open-mouthed kisses he'd given my thighs. He kissed up and down on each side, his eyes drifting closed again. His hands came into play, settling on my inner thighs to part me wider for him. His warm breath fell on me, and his tongue came out to stroke slowly. "Soft," he murmured. "So smooth and soft."

The Brazilian wax that had been part of my salon makeover now seemed totally worth the agony and embarrassment and the upkeep. The drag of Lucas's tongue over sensitized skin sent pleasure rushing through me in hot waves. Another rough, needy sound slid from my mouth.

Ben continued to play with my breasts, and he settled us deeper into the pillows. His fingers squeezed and tugged at my nipples until they felt hot and throbbing. That only heightened the echoing ache in my womb, my entire body a hot glow.

"Sweet nipples," he whispered in my ear. "Look how hard they are." He flicked one and my abdomen clenched hard in response.

Lucas gave me more slow, melting licks, his fingers separating and probing my flesh. His murmurs spoke of appreciation as he tasted me, and thick, honeyed pleasure flowed through my veins.

He slid one long finger inside me, and I clenched around that incursion, moaning again. Ben kissed my neck and shoulder as he fondled my aching breasts, and Lucas's tongue slicked over me.

Mindless with rapture, my eyes fell closed and I turned myself over to it, to the sensation, the pure delight of being the center of their attention. It was intoxicating. Addictive. Seductive.

In some corner of my mind, I recognized the risk we were taking. An inner voice was screaming, *What the fuck are you doing?* I ignored it, ignored all thoughts of what was going to happen after this, tomorrow, and every day after that when we had to work together. There was just this moment, and I was living in it.

The ache inside me deepened, a painful emptiness that needed to be filled. I needed to come, so bad. I reached for Lucas's head and slid my fingers through his thick hair. Heat coiled inside me, and I arched my back, pushing my breasts farther into Ben's palms. "God," I whispered. "Oh god. Lucas . . ."

He licked around my straining clit, teasing me unbearably. My fingers tightened in his hair. He grunted and then his tongue slid right over my clit. I jolted, hard, hips lifting.

"Oh yeah! Please . . . more . . ."

He flicked his tongue over the swollen bud again and again, a steady rhythm that my body picked up and soared with. That coiling heat tightened even more, higher, hotter. Ben's fingers pinching my nipples brought me higher still. Everything inside me pulled up taut and for a moment I was suspended on a peak of agonizing pleasure. Vaguely I knew I was making soft, whimpering, pleading sounds, and both guys were whispering lovely dirty words of encouragement.

Ben whispered in my ear. "Beautiful. Come for us, Haylee."

"Your pussy's squeezing my fingers," Lucas groaned, then resumed his tongue action on my quivering clit.

And I exploded against his mouth, with soft wails and gasps of delight, pleasure spreading from my core in hot waves. Lucas opened his mouth over my clit and sucked, prolonging the waves so they went on and on until my body went lax and boneless. I pushed at his head frantically, my clit so sensitized I couldn't bear any more. "God, stop. Can't take—"

He lifted his head, and I tried to focus my blurry vision on him. His lips were wet, his face flushed. He wiped the back of his hand across his mouth. Ben wrapped his arms around my middle, hugging me to him tightly, his face pressed to my head.

Lucas stroked my thighs. "Jesus Christ, Haylee. That was incredible."

Incredible. Yeah. That was a word. I couldn't make my lips form words, though, so I gave a tiny nod and closed my eyes, head falling back to Ben's shoulder. I breathed in shallow pants through my mouth, my arms atop Ben's around me, clutching him. I felt Lucas moving and then sensed his heat, his scent, as he came closer, then his mouth found mine for a long, sweet kiss.

"I could fucking do that all night," he whispered against my lips. "Wanna make you come again. Wanna make you come until you see stars."

"Might be there already," I managed to whisper. His mouth smiled against me.

Ben growled. "Back off, buddy. I get a turn to make her come apart."

I licked my lips, tasting myself on them. Lucas moved away, and through half-open eyes I saw them exchange another one of their looks, long and loaded. Their incomprehensible interchange fascinated me.

"Sure," Lucas drawled. "That means I get to suck on those pretty nipples."

My head still spun enough that thinking was difficult, but I figured out they apparently weren't done with me yet. My respiration was nearing normal, but my body still felt too relaxed to move. "Not sure I can take any more." I shifted in Ben's arms to turn and look at him. His dark scruffy jaw was right there. "Um . . . You guys . . ."

What the hell was I supposed to say? What was I supposed to offer in return for that incredible orgasm? Did I offer blow jobs for all? Were we actually going to all have sex together? How did that work with three people? Incredibly, my stomach did another roll of lust at these scattered thoughts.

"Relax, Haylee." Ben pressed his lips to my temple. "We only do what you want. We wanna make you feel good."

"I feel so good I can't move. But . . . that's not fair. In fact, it's weird."

They both laughed, and I couldn't help but smile too. A shiver of relief worked through me that we could all still laugh together. Because I had no frickin' clue what I was doing and where this was going and what the *hell* was going to happen tomorrow.

"You guys . . . I want you to feel good too."

Lucas's wicked eyebrow rose. "Oh yeah?"

"Yeah. I just . . ." More uncertainty overcame me. But really, at that point I would've done whatever they wanted, I think—I felt that good.

"Don't worry about us," Ben said.

"But . . . but is this how threesomes go? I think you guys should at least take your clothes off."

Once more they chuckled.

"Helluva good idea." Lucas reached behind his head to grasp his T-shirt and pull it off. He sat on the side of the bed and tugged off his boots. After they landed on the carpet with two thuds, he stood, hands at the buckle of his low-rise jeans. He was one sexy cowboy with his silver buckle and broad expanse of muscled bare chest. With masculine flicks of his wrists and fingers, he unfastened his belt and buttons and pushed the jeans down over lean hips, along with his boxers.

My eyes widened as I watched him, fascinated. Yes, I'd seen Lucas shirtless before. He had a beautiful chest, with a faint dusting of golden-brown hair between his pecs and ripped abs from his conscientious workout routine. His arms bulged with muscles too, and as my gaze dropped, I took in his narrow hips and strong thighs and . . . an enormous erection. My heart did a funny bump in my chest, and my eyelashes fluttered as if I was embarrassed or afraid to look—even though I wanted to so badly.

He gave his thick penis one stroke, and my pussy clenched hard again. Already.

He knelt on the bed and reached for me, pulling me away from Ben, up onto my knees too and then we were hugging, body to body, naked skin to naked skin and my every nerve ending sang with voluptuous pleasure. His hand curved around my neck and up into my hair, cupping the back of my head, and he kissed me.

I set my hands on his strong shoulders, opened my mouth to him, and pressed my breasts to his bare chest. Bliss blazed through my body as Lucas's fingers tangled in my hair and his tongue slid into my mouth, caressing mine.

I sensed Ben's movement off the bed as he too shed his clothing with a rustle and clink of his belt buckle. The enormity of what we were doing flickered through my mind. I was in my hotel room with two naked men! And those men were Ben and Lucas. We had totally lost our minds.

Ben's hands landed on my hips, and with a gentle tug, he drew me away from Lucas. Wide-eyed, lips parted, I stared at Lucas, and he gave me a wry smile. "Greedy bastard," he said.

"You know it," Ben murmured. "Want your mouth now, Haylee. Kiss me."

And it was his turn for a long, deep kiss. He licked into my mouth, and our tongues slid together as he wrapped his arms around me. His fingertips brushed over the top curve of my ass, then slid lower to cup me there.

"You have the sweetest ass," he murmured, kissing his way across my jaw again.

"True that." Lucas reclined on the pillows. "Spectacular. And your tits are amazing too." Was it my imagination, or were they competing to give me compliments?

"Christ, Haylee." Ben squeezed one cheek and helpless excitement rose in me again.

He found my mouth once more, and we got lost in long, drugging kisses. I swept my hands over the sleek hot skin of his shoulders and back, drew his unique scent into my lungs and tipped my pelvis into his. His cock thrust between us, long, thick, powerful. It made my inner muscles tighten all over again.

"Wanna make you come again," he whispered to me. "D'you want my fingers or my mouth?"

"Um . . . both?"

He smiled and eased me down to my back next to Lucas on the bed. Lucas immediately rolled to his side facing me and set his palm flat on my belly. "Fuck, that was hot." He sounded almost surprised. "Watching you two kiss . . . your tongues licking . . . my dick's on fire."

I swallowed. "I-I want to do something about that. Really."

He did the sexy eyebrow arch at me. "Yeah?"

I gave a tiny nod.

"Hmmm. Well, if you really want it . . ." He looked at Ben, who was parting my thighs once again. I followed his gaze and took in Ben's expression: fascinated and hungry. My insides fluttered.

At that moment, even though I'd been nearly freaking out at the idea that I was in a hotel room naked with two naked men, I realized that I had a certain power in this situation. They both seemed so captivated and so eager to please me, it made me feel feminine and beautiful and strong.

Just what I wanted.

I let myself revel in that unusual feeling, unusual for me, the tomboy, the athlete, the girl guys liked to drink beer with and talk about football with. Now I was sensual and desirable and taking so much pleasure in my body, with the attention I was receiving—their touches, their looks, their kisses.

"Fuck, Haylee." Ben stroked my pussy and shivers ran over me.

Lucas leaned closer. "See . . . so sweet." His hand slipped up my torso, between my breasts, which swelled in their desire for his touch. My nipples tingled, and as Lucas fixed his gaze on them, they tightened painfully. He pressed on my chest, fingers splayed above my breasts, his arm brushing their inner curves, and then he licked his lips and bent his head. His eyelids lowered and his tongue came out to tease over one nipple.

It wasn't enough. I shuddered, but I needed more. He licked again, then took my nipple into his mouth. With gentle suction, he had my abdominal muscles contracting hard and my pussy squeezing. A moan climbed up my throat.

I lifted one hand to his head, and my other rose then flopped to the bed.

"You know what would be good?" Lucas murmured, lifting his head.

"Wh-what?"

"You, tied up."

Heat flashed through me, and I sucked in a breath. My eyes flew open to meet his.

He grinned. "Yeah. Tied up and helpless. So all you can do is let us make you feel good."

My mouth dropped open. "Tied up?"

"Great idea," Ben mumbled, just before he put his mouth on me.

Fuuuuck! My hips lifted and everything inside me twisted with excitement.

Tied up! Oh holy crumb cakes! And Ben was licking me, sending sizzles through my veins. Lucas tugged harder on one nipple with his mouth, and I gave a strangled cry. Sensation streamed from there to where Ben's tongue licked, and I strained toward him for more, more, please more . . . I realized I was babbling that aloud.

"Yeah, sweetheart." Ben touched his tongue to my throbbing clit. "More."

Ben's hands and fingers on my breasts and nipples had been wonderful, but now Lucas sucking on me too was . . . sensational. I'd never experienced anything like that . . . How could you, with only one man, one mouth? Two was incredible!

"I want you to both suck my nipples," I demanded breathlessly, shocking myself. "Please," I added.

Ben lifted his head. "Oh yeah, I can do that." He crawled closer, and then he and Lucas each took a nipple into their mouths.

Oh dear god. My back arched, my fingers curled into fists, and a sharp ache materialized low in my belly. Never, never, ever had I felt something so erotic, so excruciatingly delicious. My hands cupped their heads, holding them at my breasts as they tugged and sucked on the tender tips. God. Oh god.

My chin lifted, head going back deeper into the pillow, waves of pleasure washing over me. My pussy tightened and begged for more.

"It's so good," I gasped. "So good. But not enough."

"You need to come, baby," Ben mumbled against my breast. He tenderly licked over the nipple, gave nibbling kisses to the curves around it, then dragged his tongue along the underside of my breast. My hips lifted off the bed again.

"Yes. Yes." But I knew I needed more than just an orgasm, I needed to be filled, needed to be . . . fucked. Oh god. Could I ask for that? Would they do that? What we were doing was crazy, but actually fucking . . .

Ben slipped his hand down my body and between my legs, cupping my pulsing pussy. His big fingers stroked through my folds, all slick and wet. Then he brushed over my clit, and I jerked hard.

"Yeah," he murmured. "So hot."

I lifted my head to look at them, their heads so close together, almost touching. I saw Ben's gaze shift sideways to watch Lucas sucking my nipple. I went mindless and a little crazy. Ben's finger again found my clit and started a circular motion over it. I shifted just a tiny . . . tiny . . . bit . . . to get it on the exact . . . right . . . spot . . . *there*. "Oh god, yes, there . . ." Sensations began to converge inside me, hot and tight, almost painful in their intensity.

I dug my heels into the mattress and pushed up into Ben's hand. His fingers were good, so good, applying just the right pressure. He read my slight movements and responses to know just where to touch. I could have cried, it was so incredible, and I was stunned at the emotion that rose from my chest up my throat, nearly choking me.

My hips lifted restlessly, searchingly, and a huge lovely swell rose inside me, rushing hot and pure. I cried out as I came, my fingers clutching two male heads to my breasts.

Ben's fingers stilled on my pussy, cupping me gently as I pulsed against his palm. Holy fuck. Holy fucking fuck. This was off the charts hot. Never, never, never. Fragments of thoughts spun around in my head as I whimpered and sucked in air, and my chest heaved. They both drew away and took turns gently kissing my mouth, my cheeks, my neck.

"Guys," I moaned. "Oh my god, guys, you killed me."

"Oh baby," Ben said, hand still between my legs. "That was nothin'."

"I don't think I could survive anything more." I said it because I thought it, but the truth was—I *wanted* more.

But I was also exhausted. Limp. Replete. The emotional intensity of the concert, the alcohol, and two stunning orgasms had drained my energy. My eyes were heavy, my body lethargic. Drowsiness crept over me, rendering me even more lax.

I petted their heads, Lucas's thick hair, Ben's silky soft. "You guys. You guys." I knew I babbled, but it was all I could manage. "So sweet. I love you guys."

Yeah, that might've been a stupid thing to say. They knew what I meant. I hoped. Just then I was too overcome with lethargy and sleep to try to clarify. So I closed my eyes and drifted off, barely waking when the soft duvet was pulled up over me.

CHAPTER 5
DIDN'T KNOW WHAT I WANTED WAS GONNA BE SO HARD
AND I DON'T WANT TO LOSE THIS.

I woke up the next morning groggy, blinking into the dark hotel room. The blinds shut out all light, and I had no idea what time it was. I turned my head on the pillow to see the digital alarm clock. Ten fifteen. Huh.

Memories began to sift through my morning fog. Last night . . . Ben and Lucas . . . oh my god. My head whipped back around, but I was alone in the king-sized bed.

I stared up at the ceiling for long moments, trying to figure out if I'd had some crazy dreams last night or if what I remembered had really happened. Oh my god. I squeezed my eyes shut at the rush of heat through my body. Oh my god.

My stomach knotted, and I rolled to my side, knees bent up to my chest, face buried in a pillow. I was never going to leave this bed. Never going to face the world. And especially never going to face Lucas and Ben again. I would go to Alaska. No . . . Kazakhstan.

Which pretty much meant my country music career was over.

I briefly contemplated the extent of the country music business in Kazakhstan, but then I started to hyperventilate. My head went light and spinny. My heart missed a beat, raced, missed another beat. I broke out in a sweat.

Then I heard a knock on the door.

My eyes flew open wide. Not gonna answer it. Whoever it was. Not going there.

But then I heard a click, and I bolted upright, grabbing the duvet to my naked body. Someone was coming in. Maybe room service . . .

Lucas appeared, Ben close behind him.

Oh my god, oh my god. I stared at them, clutching the duvet in front of my chest.

"How'd you get in?" I croaked.

Lucas held up the key card between two fingers. "We borrowed this when we left."

My teeth nibbled at my bottom lip. The room was still whirling slightly. "Wh-when did you leave?"

Lucas glanced at Ben and shrugged. "Around two, I think. When you crashed on us."

Oh. Yeah. His gently accusing tone made me blink. "I guess I did crash. Um . . ." Was I supposed to apologize? I bit my lip again, remembering that I'd wanted more, so much more, and they'd been aroused and . . . had gotten nothing in return. It had bothered me last night, and I still felt guilty about that. God! This was surreal!

Dressed in worn jeans, boots, and a T-shirt that hugged his broad chest, Lucas advanced on the bed. "You passed out before we got to the good stuff. Leaving us hanging, high and dry and horny. But you can make it up to us tonight." He winked.

Tonight! Holy crapsickle! My eyes widened, and my insides did a flip. My gaze darted to Ben, who regarded me with an expressionless face, hands shoved into the pockets of his jeans. His button-down shirt was untucked, worn with a skinny tie and a cotton blazer.

"We wanted to make sure you were up in time to get to the

airport," he said quietly. "It's nearly ten thirty."

Lucas nodded. "I was afraid maybe you'd gotten up and put the privacy lock on."

"I just woke up." I sat up straighter and tried for a glare. "Ever think of maybe just knocking on my door?"

Lucas grinned. "We did knock."

"You didn't give me time to answer!"

My eyes widened as he sat on the bed. "Wasn't sure how you were going to react today, babe."

"You okay, Haylee?" Ben stayed away from the bed, his shoulders tight. Our eyes met, but his were shuttered. His concern for me touched me, but I studied his face, a little concerned about *him*. He seemed . . . quiet. Distant. Was he in one of his moods? Was he regretting what we'd done?

"I'm okay," I managed to say. My face burned.

Lucas laid his big hand on my shoulder. "You were amazing." He trailed his fingertips down my upper arm.

My heart crashed against my ribs. I swear all the oxygen in the room disappeared because I could not breathe. Somehow I managed to choke out some words. "I-I was amazing?" I'd done nothing! They were the ones who'd done everything. They'd given me more pleasure in one night than Doug had in six months, not to mention two of the most intense orgasms of my life. Holy hotness!

Lucas leaned over and kissed my lips, softly, sweetly. "We need to get packed, grab breakfast, and get to the airport, gorgeous."

I blinked. Several times. "Uh. Yeah. I guess we do."

He'd called me gorgeous.

Ben stood watching us, saying nothing. Then he asked, "Sure you're okay, Haylee?"

I wanted to scream, *No, I'm not okay! Freaking out, here! What have we done?* Lucas apparently wanted to pick up where we'd left off, and Ben did not. Freaking out was right. But I kept my lips pressed firmly together and nodded.

They exchanged looks, which was becoming a regular thing. Actually, it always had been. They'd always been able to communicate wordlessly, but usually when it came to music. The rest of the time their communication consisted of trash talk and insults. Now they seemed to be communicating about me, and I wasn't sure if I liked it. This look was charged with . . . something I couldn't read.

"I was afraid of this," Ben muttered.

Lucas sighed and shoved a hand through his hair. I remembered only too well what that felt like, his thick, soft hair . . . My respiration sped up again, and I started to panic even more.

Lucas frowned. "Hey," he said. "You look like you need a paper bag over your face."

I frowned at him. "What the hell does that mean?"

"For your breathing. Relax." He edged closer, and his hand rubbed my back in a slow rhythm. "Relax, babe. It's okay."

I pulled the duvet up over my head. Lucas's soft chuckle permeated the thick layer. His hand continued its soothing strokes, and the darkness and probably lack of oxygen eased my panic.

Gentle hands tugged the duvet away from my face. Lucas handed me my tank top and pajama shorts. "Here. Put these on. We'll talk later. We need to get moving."

Okay, enough of the sweet stuff. He was back to take-charge Lucas.

Ben gave Lucas a long look as Lucas rose off the bed, then turned his gaze back to me, the skin around his eyes tight, his lips set into a straight line.

The room spun as it had the night before after the drinks I'd had. Yep, freaking right the hell out. I tried to gather my thoughts and get control of my trembling body. I sucked in a long breath and fumbled beneath the covers to tug on the shorts. When it came to putting on the tank top, it seemed ridiculous to hide beneath the covers when they'd seen everything I had, and that meant *everything*. So I dropped the duvet and pulled on the top, my breasts tightening as I knew they watched. I swung my legs over the side of the bed and sat there for a moment. "Okay," I said. "I need to get dressed and pack."

We were going home. Home to Nashville. After being on the road for so long, I'd been looking forward to getting back to our house and normal life, and back to writing and recording. But now . . . How normal could things be? My heart kept up that fast, frantic rhythm.

"We'll meet you in the lobby for breakfast," Lucas said, heading for the door. "How long? Ten minutes?"

I resisted the urge to roll my eyes. Ten minutes to get ready? Clearly he knew how low-maintenance I was. "I'm not really hungry. I'm just going to get packed. You guys go on and have breakfast without me."

Lucas nodded. "Okay, sure, babe. We'll be back."

They left me alone again. I still sat on the edge of the bed, hands planted beside me. I looked down at my toes, all professionally pedicured with peony-pink polish. Well. This was mortifying. Lucas's cocky assumption that we'd be doing it again that night made my insides do another slow roll of lust, even as it terrified me. On the other hand, I got the feeling Ben wasn't so eager. Confusion twisted up inside me as I considered rushing to the phone to change my flight.

No. How could I run from them when we lived together? Somehow we'd have to deal with this.

I rose from the bed. I'd better get busy.

I hit the shower, then searched for clothes. It was a travel day, so I dressed in my favorite faded low-rise jeans and a T-shirt—but, acknowledging the fact that there could be photographers anywhere, the T-shirt was a silky slub-knit white with silvery graphics on the front, my boots were bronze-and-black Lucchese, and I added a small fitted jacket in charcoal, super-soft leather.

When I went to do my makeup I expected to look like hell, but strangely, once I faced myself in the mirror, it wasn't that bad. I'd slept like crazy after . . . well, *after*. And even though I might have drunk a teensy bit too much last night, I looked okay. I took inventory of how I felt: I didn't feel hungover. My thighs felt tight, which reminded me of lying with them spread apart while Ben and Lucas pleasured me. Heat curled low in my belly and my nipples tightened, clearly visible through the thin T-shirt; color washed into my cheeks. Huh. I actually looked . . . good.

I dried my hair, did a quick run over with the flat iron, and added mascara to my pale eyelashes and some gloss to my lips. Then I paused and slowly pulled out an eye shadow compact. As I applied more makeup and tousled my hair, it struck me that I wanted to look nice for Lucas and Ben. Crazysauce.

I'd become an expert packer even though it was tedious, so I soon had my suitcases neatly filled and zipped up, ready to go. I was scanning the room for any overlooked items when someone knocked on the door again.

This time I expected it to be Lucas and Ben, though I peeked through the peephole to make sure before opening the door. Ben held out a huge cardboard cup of coffee and a small bag. "Here."

I took them automatically, my mouth watering at the scent of rich, dark coffee. I shot him a grateful look. "Thank you."

"I know you need your morning caffeine."

I felt an urge to kiss him, but he stepped back. Kissing him was a crazy idea anyway.

Ben pointed to the bag. "And we got you a bagel. You'll starve if you don't eat something before we leave."

He was right, dammit. My lips pursed as I nodded.

"All packed?" Lucas started toward my suitcases, then gave me an up-and-down appraisal that heated my skin. "You look great."

Oh my god, what was going on here? "Thank you," I choked out. "And yes, I'm ready."

"The car's waiting. Our stuff's already down there. Let's go."

I slung my big slouchy purse over my shoulder and clutched my coffee and bagel as the guys grabbed my cases, and we headed down to the lobby.

We were at about thirty thousand feet, through our Chicago connection and well on our way to Nashville, when I couldn't stand it anymore. The guys had both wanted to sit beside me, and since I didn't really care where I was seated and it made them happy, I sat between them in the row of three seats. I was acutely aware of their long legs and muscular thighs on either side of me, their broad shoulders brushing mine. Lucas kept talking about anything and everything—the tour, the concert last night, our plans for resuming work, song ideas, not to mention flirting like crazy with me—but didn't seem to notice that Ben and I were not really responding. In fact, the scowl Ben wore had the flight attendant casting him uneasy glances.

I was one of those people who needed some alone time. Ben and I were both like that. We loved performing, but there were definitely times we needed to recharge our batteries. Ben had a moody side to him. When he needed some solitude, he got grouchy. I think I might have been the only person who ever pointed that out to him, because he'd scowled at me, seeming surprised the first time I told him to take a break and go build something by himself. Then he'd laughed. He was really critical of himself, down on himself if he didn't play his best or made a mistake, and it made me feel good to make him laugh. Which I apparently did without even trying.

Lucas, on the other hand, fed off the energy of people around him, almost high on it after a concert. We'd had to clue him in pretty early on to the fact that he couldn't expect to hang around us every minute of every day, because as much as we loved him, that would suck the life out of us.

47

This was one of those times.

I took a deep breath. "Lucas."

"Yeah?"

"You need to stop talking."

He blinked at me.

"Ben." I turned to him. "Put your earbuds in and listen to some music. You're acting all broody."

Ben's eyebrows lowered and his mouth tightened even more. Then he let out a breath. "Yeah." He pulled out his iPhone. I did the same. I tried to let music soothe me for the rest of the flight, and it helped somewhat, but my stomach was still fluttering wildly thinking about what had happened and what was apparently going to happen again.

Brandon had arranged a car service to take us home when we landed in Nashville. It was a short drive from the airport on I-40, then onto Briley Parkway, then McGavock Pike where our house was. When we'd started to have some success, somehow the idea had been broached that the three of us should move into Ben's house. I'd been living in a dumpy apartment, and Lucas'd had a downtown condo that he hated. It made perfect sense that we share Ben's big house. He'd bought it mainly for the huge garage where he'd run his carpentry business. He'd gotten a good deal on the house because it needed so much work, but since that was his trade, he'd had no problem doing the renos on it. It had five bedrooms, four bathrooms, studio space for us to work, a living room and a main-floor family room, so we could all easily have our own space when we needed.

In the backseat of the car, my insides twisted into knots as we sped along I-40. But I couldn't keep it in any longer. "Okay. We need to talk."

"Now?" Lucas glanced at the driver, then back at me. "You want to talk *now*? We're almost home."

I nibbled the nail on my index finger. "I'm sorry, but I really need to know . . . what's going on."

He gave me an incredulous look, then took my hand. "You have to ask? Haylee, you have to admit . . . this has been building up for a while."

"It has?" I blinked.

His forehead creased. "Hell yeah. You can't tell me you haven't felt it. There's always been chemistry between us."

Ben sighed. "Fuck."

Lucas shot him a look. "All of us."

"For making music!" Oops, that came out kind of loud. "Not for . . ."

Lucas bent over to whisper in my ear. "Sex."

Ben sighed again. I tried to ignore him for the moment. "If you mean last night on stage—"

"Yeah, that was hot." Lucas tightened his fingers over mine. "But it wasn't just last night."

My head whirled yet again. I was *so* not their type of girl. But I had to admit, last night in bed, that hadn't seemed to matter one bit. I swiped my tongue across my lips and watched Lucas's eyes lower to my mouth. I felt a dart of heat low in my belly.

Hmm.

My body tingled, and I was seized with anticipation of what was going to happen once we were home.

"You can make it up to us later," Lucas had said.

Remembering their strong, muscled bodies and how patient and attentive they'd been to me, and how I'd wanted to give them the same kind of pleasure, heat poured over me. I blinked rapidly and reached for the button that lowered the window, then shoved my face into the cool air that rushed into the car.

Lucas chuckled. "Is it horny in here, or is it just you?"

That got a laugh from Ben, and I had to join in, some of the tension easing out of me. I tightened my fingers on his hand. Ben sat on the other side of Lucas, and I wished I could hold his hand too. These two guys confused me and made me hot, but they also made me laugh. It was the craziest thing. Last night had just happened, spontaneously (sort of), fueled by a little alcohol (maybe), but anything that happened tonight, I was not going to be able to blame on a little booze and involuntary, uncontrollable lust.

I didn't have to do it. If I told them I wasn't into casual sex, or threesomes, or any kind of sexual relationship with the guys who were my bandmates—what would happen? Would we still be able to work together?

I nibbled my bottom lip, letting the cool air rush over my heated face.

My career was important to me. Music was my life. I'd started singing and playing guitar as a kid, with my dad's band, traveling with him from town to town. I'd left home right after high school, against my dad's wishes, and moved to Los Angeles, determined to have a bigger career than you could have in North Dakota. In LA, it had taken a few years of waitressing, walking dogs, and telemarketing before I actually got somewhere, singing backup vocals and actually selling some of my songs. But I'd also realized LA wasn't for me.

I'd been avoiding writing country music, rebelling against the traditional country songs my dad's band played, simple three-chord numbers about downer topics like drowning sorrows in a bottle of Jack. But when B.J. Avery had recorded a song I'd written, adding pedal steel and fiddle, it had been a huge country hit, and I'd decided to move to Nashville and see what would happen.

I'd soon met Lucas, who was also writing. We met at the Bluebird Café during one of their writers' nights. I'd really liked what he was doing. I'd introduced myself and boldly suggested that we collaborate, and amazingly he took me up on my offer. And that was when the magic had started.

Lucas already knew Ben and invited him to help us record some of our demos. Lucas and I were both fair guitarists, but Ben's guitar and fiddle skills were amazing. I played keyboard, rounding out our little band, although I could also play guitar. When we'd listened to the demo with my throaty contralto, Lucas's bass, and Ben's smooth background vocals singing three-part harmony, we'd all sat there and stared at each other. Were we nuts, or did we have something unique and special?

Apparently we *did* have something unique and special, given how fast things had clicked for us after that. I didn't have the best voice in the business, but the three of us together created a fresh new sound. Alone, I was a good singer. Together . . . well, I'm not bragging when I say we sounded great.

When I thought about what I'd accomplished so far, pride swelled inside me. When I thought about what Ben and Lucas and I had created together, the success we were having, the possibilities that lay before us, it blew my mind.

I did not want to lose all that.

The idea that we might have screwed up something so incredible made my heart race so fast I thought it might explode.

The smart thing would be to tell them no. To talk about how it would be a mistake to mix up sex with business. Because even though music was my love, I firmly considered what we did to be business. We were all professional musicians and that was one reason we got along so well. We all took it seriously, we were all committed, and we all wanted the same things.

But yeah, there was chemistry . . . there was a whole shipload of chemistry. I'd always known it. In my head, all along, it was musical chemistry—it was how we collaborated on songs that hit the charts, sold out concerts, and started rumors that Lucas and I were a couple.

But maybe I'd been blind. Or in denial. Because the chemistry was definitely sexual. And I was about to do something crazy and wicked and hot as all damn hell.

CHAPTER 6
PART OF ME WANTS TO STOP,
PART OF ME WANTS TO GO . . .

We all headed straight to our bedrooms to unpack and change when we got home. But unpacking seemed overwhelming just then. I had laundry to do and dry cleaning to drop off. I had emails to go through and voice mails to check. All I wanted to do was change into sweats and crash on a couch with a beer and some music on the stereo, but I had two hot guys to deal with.

I ignored my suitcases and changed into loose sweats which I rolled down on my hips. I reached for my Nashville Predators hoodie, but then wrinkled my nose remembering I'd bought it because of Doug.

Holy bejeebus, I hadn't thought of Doug all day. Now, remembering what had happened just yesterday merely annoyed me, instead of stinging hard like it had. My lip curled. Asshole. I clearly was better off without him.

What would Doug think if he knew what had happened in my hotel room last night? I remembered once Doug had complained about the time I spent with Ben and Lucas, with all these questions about what happened on the road, as if he was jealous or suspicious of us. I remembered him saying he didn't like the way Lucas looked

at me, and I'd laughed at him, thinking his distrust was ridiculous
—*as if* those two guys would look at me any other way than as their
partner and buddy, when they had hot groupies hanging off them!
But that had been then, and—wow, things had, um, changed. So
there, Doug Brandt! Except now he probably didn't even care.

Sadly, I liked watching hockey, which I'd learned to love growing
up in North Dakota, and I'd been a Predators fan for a while before
I'd met Doug. Hopefully I'd be able to go to games without being
bummed about him.

I grabbed another hoodie, a soft Tennessee Titans one. I pulled
my hair back into a ponytail and headed for the kitchen, undeniably
hungry now.

I still couldn't really believe Lucas meant it when he'd said I was
supposed to make up to them for what hadn't happened last night.
My insides did a flip of excitement. Last night had been really, really
hot, and I'd felt really, really sexy for one of the few times in my life.
Despite my misgivings, I wanted that again.

Then I looked down at myself. Oh yeah. I was dressed for seduc-
tion all right. I stopped at my bedroom door, a small battle waging
inside my head. Last night I'd been all glammed up. Was that why
that had happened? Should I go change?

Nah. That was stupid. If I dressed up, it would look ridiculous.
That wasn't me. I was learning to present an image to the rest of the
world, but in my own home with Ben and Lucas, I was just me—
jeans and boots, sweats and hoodies. If I looked like I was trying too
hard, they'd fall over laughing.

Whatever. I was hungry.

In the kitchen, I surveyed our empty refrigerator. Uh-oh. This
might be a problem. My favorite Greek yogurt was a month past the
best-before date. All that was there besides that was ketchup,
mustard, margarine, and a jar of pickles. And one lonely, lovely
beer.

The cupboards were marginally better. We had boxes of pasta

and a can of tomato sauce, so I could put those together. But first, I pulled out an unopened can of my favorite snack, peanuts. God, I love peanuts.

With my peanuts and beer, I headed to the living room. I switched on the gas fireplace—Ben turned his nose up at it, thinking it should be wood burning, but that was how the house had been built. As the fire warmed up the room, I started the stereo with a playlist queued up from my iPod—Alison Krauss and Lee Ann Womack, Eric Clapton, and Eddie Van Halen.

My home—or should I say, *our* home—was my refuge from the constant action and travel and interaction. Yes, I spent hours on the computer doing promotional work. I spent nearly as much time on the charity work I was involved with, raising money for Children's Hospital at Vanderbilt, and for Parker Home, an after-school program for at-risk kids. But home was where I refilled my creative well, with quiet time and listening to favorite music that inspired me, stretched me.

I leaned my head back and let the music surround me.

Other words started filling my head, though, thoughts and feelings. Last night . . . Sweet heat swept over me.

You make me feel so beautiful . . . You make me feel so right . . . You make me burn and want to fly, you make me smile and make me sigh.

I got up, turned off the stereo, and padded in my sock feet across the hardwood floor to my baby grand piano—my prize possession—in what should have been the dining room. I sat down and opened the lid, let my fingers stroke the keys. Eyes closed, I heard the rhythm of the words and the melody, and I began to play. *Adagio.* Slow and soft. I let my hands play and my fingers sought out the right chord progressions until I had it right, then I reached for the pencil and paper I always kept nearby and began to put the song to paper with my right hand, while the left was still finding notes.

It was always best when I didn't have to try, when it was fun, and pleasure rushed through me as the music just came to me.

I shouldn't want these things, especially from you. I've never felt this way before. Your touch, your smile, your arms around me, make me feel so beautiful. Waited all my life, wanted so much more . . . Didn't know what I wanted was gonna be so hard, and I don't want to lose this.

"Hey, sweetheart. Whatcha doin'?"

I blinked into the dark room. I'd become lost in the song, and now the lamp over the piano and the fireplace in the living room provided the only light. Whoa.

Ben was standing there.

I held up my pad of paper. "Writing."

He looked at me for a long moment, and I sensed that disquietude still inside him. "Let's hear it."

I stared down at the piano keys, pure white and black, so smooth and beautiful. For the first time ever, I found myself shy to share with him what I'd written. It felt so personal—yet the best songs were the ones that came from the heart and the soul, deep inside. Music was so sacred and powerful . . . a way to express emotion, a voyage of discovery and change, a celebration. I'd learned so much about myself through music, and I knew there was more to discover.

So I played what I had so far, and sang the words. It wasn't a complete song; I wasn't even sure at that point if it was something that would work.

Ben picked up a guitar and made me sing it again as he played, adding chords, making it richer.

The *ping* of the door alarm sounded as someone entered the house, and then the scent of spicy tomato sauce, sausage, and melted cheese reached my nose.

Lucas appeared holding a huge pizza and a twelve-pack of beer. He set them down and joined Ben and me, listening, and then he hummed with me when I sang the words *fill me up with wanting more.* There was only a short pause before he sang back to me, *more love.*

Our eyes met.

He tilted his head as if listening, but the room was silent. I knew he was hearing music in his head. He nodded slowly, his mouth soft and lovely, eyes heavy lidded. The air went electric around all of us, and I shivered, which meant something beautiful was happening. It had happened before. Then Lucas straightened. "Yeah." His voice was husky. "I got it. That's the chorus."

I handed him my pencil and staff paper, but he shook his head. "It's okay. I got it."

I wasn't sure what he had, but I just nodded.

"Let's eat," he said. "I'm starving."

Ben set down his guitar, and I could see that his shoulders had lost some of their tension. The power of music. I felt calmer also.

My hands rested on my thighs, and I gave both guys a slow smile. "Yeah. Me too."

We all moved to the kitchen, and I found plates and glasses. "I didn't know you'd gone out to get food. Things were a wee bit sparse in the cupboards."

Lucas cracked open a beer. "I know. And no one feels like cooking our first night back."

"I would like a home cooked meal," I said wistfully, sliding a piece of pizza onto my plate, "sometime."

We loaded up with pizza and poured beers. Then we headed into the living room, where we often ate in front of the television.

Ben and Lucas set their plates and drinks on the coffee table. I was going to sit on one of the armchairs since they'd each taken an end of the couch, but Lucas patted the cushion between them, so I sat there. Ben grabbed the TV remote and found a football game.

It wasn't the first time we'd ever done this, and the familiarity of it only served to make last night more absurdly dreamlike. There was no way we were going from this—pizza, beer, and foot-ball—to hot ménage à trois sex. This was just too normal and platonic.

Or maybe I was in denial.

Except it wasn't really platonic, because sitting shoulder to shoulder with them on the couch made my skin tingle. Shivery sensation shimmered over me and heat built around us.

Lucas started talking about the song. "It's got two parts. You start with the first verse, I sing the second, we sing the third together. I know just how it's going to go."

"I'm glad *you* do."

He grinned and lifted his pizza to his mouth.

My mind didn't want to let the song go yet. "It needs a hook."

"We'll get it," Ben put in.

"I don't even know what it's about."

Lucas's eyes met mine. "I do."

Heat crawled from my neck up into my face.

Lucas shook his head. "Relax, baby."

"I am relaxed."

"Uh-huh."

He knew I was lying. He knew my insides were tight and my breasts were heavy and I was all distracted and perturbed.

I looked down at my beer. "We can work on it tomorrow."

Ben leaned his shoulder into mine. "We just got home, and you're gonna make us work already?"

"Oh. Sorry. I know you guys wanted time off over Christmas . . ." I bit my lip.

"We'll work on the song," Lucas said firmly.

"When did you get so bossy?"

"Babe. Always have been. Are you seriously just noticing now?"

I tipped my head to one side. "You have a point."

At my concession, his eyes crinkled up.

Yes, Lucas was the unofficial leader of our group. Not that Ben and I let him walk all over us. We'd had more than one heated argument over music, staging, business decisions . . . all kinds of things. Lucas was the one who liked being in control and making decisions, confident in his thinking and strong willed. I was equally driven and had my own stubborn streak, but in our two years together I'd learned how to sneak past his single-mindedness and get him to occasionally admit there might be another way. And even though I argued with him, sometimes it felt good to have someone that strong and sure of himself leading the way for us. At times when I was doubtful or questioning what we were doing, it made me feel secure and safe in our path. And weirdly, with his focus and determination to succeed, I felt good when I could make him laugh too.

Ben sighed.

Lucas cast him an amused glance. "You know it's not work, you fucking love it as much as I do."

"Yeah, yeah, fine. But we're both leaving Christmas Eve."

I shrugged. "I'll be here. I'll be working."

"We could all use a break," Lucas said quietly. "I think *you* could use a break." He eyed me, and I blinked.

"It's in my head, and I need to get it out." I needed to get the song out so I could share it with the world. Lucas was right. It wasn't work. I loved it.

They both smiled, knowing exactly what I was talking about. "Even though we're done with the tour, things are still busy." Ben dropped a pizza crust onto his plate. "Lots of business to catch up on."

Lucas nodded. "Party at Brandon's place. And the gig we've got lined up at the Ryman. Jesus, who booked us for the day before Christmas Eve?"

I sighed. "Brandon did." My gut twisted into knots at the idea of singing Christmas songs. But I had to do it. For the band. For Ben and Lucas.

Ben shook his head. "Christ."

"I know. And you guys can't even leave to go home until Christmas Eve because of that gig."

"Eh, it's okay. It's a great opportunity."

Lucas focused on the TV. "Whoa. Look at that."

We all leaned forward to watch the Titans' player run with the ball for a touchdown.

"Samson really has a nose for the ball," the TV announcer shouted. The other commentator jumped in with, "He sure does, and he's the first to jump on any loose balls."

I snickered and earned amused glances from both guys.

"Mind out of the gutter, babe." Lucas nudged me.

"I can't help it! Those announcers are always saying dirty things. 'Football is a game of inches.' 'He's got great hands.'"

They both laughed.

"Last week one of the announcers was talking about penetration in the backfield and Haylee cracked up." Ben smirked and leaned in closer. "I kinda like your dirty mind."

I lowered my chin, still smiling. "Oh yeah?" Holy touchdown, I sounded flirty. What the hell?

"A dirty mind is a terrible thing to waste," Lucas said with a nod, leaning closer too. Suddenly the air I was breathing felt hot. Lucas's gaze dropped, and his eyebrows pulled together. "Nice outfit, by the way."

Was that sarcastic? Fuck, I *should* have changed into something girly. "Um . . . sorry . . ."

"Sorry for what?" He hooked a finger into the neckline of my hoodie and tugged me closer. "You're cute." He brushed his lips across my cheek. A shudder worked up my spine. "Think it's time to finish what we didn't get to last night."

CHAPTER 7

BUT YOU MAKE ME FEEL SO BEAUTIFUL,

YOU MAKE ME FEEL SO RIGHT.

The kisses were long and lush, first Lucas's mouth on mine, then Ben's. When Ben turned my face toward his, I met his eyes questioningly, still unsure how he felt about this. He gazed back at me for a long moment, then closed his eyes and groaned. He slid his hand around the back of my head and pulled me to his mouth. My head spun at the wickedness of that, of kissing two guys one after the other, and also maybe with relief that Ben still wanted me too.

While Ben's tongue slid into my mouth and played with mine, Lucas kissed the back of my neck beneath my ponytail, slowly drawing the band off and then filtering his hands through my hair. When Ben's teeth nipped my bottom lip, Lucas's hands slipped beneath my sweatshirt and caressed my back and waist. When Lucas's hand found my breast, Ben's hand was between my legs, rubbing my aching pussy through the fabric of my sweats.

I wanted to touch them too. I dug my fingers into Lucas's biceps, explored Ben's hard chest, and ran my tongue along his bearded jaw. I breathed in their scents and let my fingers slide through thick hair down to the nape of Lucas's neck, soft and tender. I gripped Ben's muscled thigh as he sucked my bottom lip.

We sat there making out, the television somehow muted and flickering silently in the dim room, the only sounds our low moans and sighs and clinging mouths. Pleasure flowed through me, thick and sweet, and I felt my body dissolving.

A long time later, Ben murmured in my ear: "You call it, Haylee. Here? Or your room?"

I found I didn't want to make that decision, as much as I appreciated the offer. "I don't know . . ."

His hands tightened on my waist. "Haylee . . . tonight we only go as far as you want."

I turned to look at him, comforted by his steady eyes and by the fact he'd once again cared enough to reassure me.

"Yeah," Lucas added, and I turned back to him. For once his usual crooked smile was absent, and he, too, held my gaze. "If you don't want to do this, just say the word." He searched my face with his eyes.

Yes, I had doubts and reservations about this, but after sitting there and kissing them until my head spun and I ached way down low inside, I couldn't make myself put a stop to it. I could no more explain this than I could explain quantum electrochemistry. I only knew what I felt, including a swelling warmth in my chest toward both of them.

I managed to whisper the word, "Bed."

Lucas gave a low growl. "Yeah. My girl deserves a bed."

"*Our* girl." Ben gave Lucas a narrow-eyed look.

Our girl?

"Right." Lucas surged up off the couch, turned and grabbed my hands, and hauled me up too. I went flying, given his bigger size and strength.

"Easy, dude." Ben stood too, his hands on my hips. He gave me a nudge toward the bedroom. Lucas tugged me along by my hands, Ben close behind.

This wasn't the first time they'd seen my bedroom. They'd

helped me paint the walls taupe, the trim white. The whole house had shiny hardwood floors, and I had a patterned rug in my room. A chocolate-brown duvet covered my bed, which had a white-painted headboard and footboard. Unfortunately the bed was only a queen-size and as soon as all three of us were on it, it was clear we were going to be forced into a lot closer proximity than in the king-size hotel bed last night.

But really, how much closer could you get than . . .

My stomach swooped. "Can we take a minute?" I sat in the middle of the bed, the guys on either side, reaching for me.

They paused. Ben searched my face, his eyes dark, endless blue. "Sure, sweetheart. Second thoughts?"

"I think this might have been a . . . mistake."

They stared at me, then Ben cursed. "Shit. You *were* drunk."

"No, I wasn't!" My eyes widened. "Well, maybe a bit. But last night, I knew exactly what I was doing. I—" I cleared my throat. "I wanted it. But I didn't expect it to happen again."

"Why not, Haylee?" Ben stroked my hair back.

"I still don't understand how you guys can want this. If you really think it through. I mean, look at me." I caught the perplexed crease on Lucas's brow.

"Uh . . . yeah. We do," he said. "Not sure why you think we don't. We're here." He swept out a hand.

"Last night . . . that was the onstage version of me—hair and makeup all done, wearing a sexy dress. But the tour is done now."

They both gave me blank looks.

"Yeah. So?" Lucas said.

"Seriously? You still want me . . . like this?" I swept a hand up and down in front of me.

Ben groaned. "So fucking much. What are you talking about, Haylee?"

I bit my lip. "I'm not . . . girly. Sexy."

"Are you fucking kidding me?" Lucas's forehead furrowed.

"That's not what last night was about. Wearing a sexy dress and makeup. Jesus fuck."

Ben's forehead creased. "You're always sexy, Haylee."

I bit my lip. They really seemed to mean it. "Thanks." Okay then. "But how do we do this? Us—this—I just don't know . . . how to do this."

"We'll show you, babe." Lucas touched my cheek. "All you have to do is enjoy yourself."

"But—"

His lips touched mine. "You did great last night. Just let us show you how good it can be."

It *had* been good. I'd been swept away, caught up in it. I'd also been a teensy bit drunk, which I was not now. I felt like I needed something more, though; some part of me needed words and explanations and reassurance. I don't know what I expected them to say. Clearly, a threesome wasn't a declaration of undying love, or a commitment to forever. And I wasn't looking for those things. So I kept my mouth shut and decided to do what Lucas said, and let them show me how good it could be.

I could do this. I could just let myself be a physical being, focused only on carnal pleasure. Sexual. Maybe even desirable. And I could deal with whatever happened after.

With a sense of déjà vu, I reached for the hem of my big sweatshirt and pulled it up over my head.

I wasn't wearing a bra and just like last night, both guys made noises of appreciation as I bared myself to them.

Ben bent his head and kissed my shoulder. "That's it, baby."

"I just want to say," I managed to wheeze out, "that it would give me pleasure to um . . . give you guys pleasure too."

Lucas nodded. "Got it. Fuck, Haylee, you have gorgeous tits."

I never would have thought such crude words would please me so much. Lucas and Ben could put together the most beautiful lyrics —sensual and lovely and poetic—but I liked how they kept it real in bed. Hearing lyrical poetry from them in bed would probably make me collapse into giggles.

As it was, everything they said was raw and real and hot, and I loved it.

Just like I loved what Ben said next. "And let's see that pretty pussy again. Christ, I haven't been able to stop thinking about you with your legs spread for us, all hot and wet." It sounded like the words were being dragged out of him, a reluctant admission.

My insides went all soft and mushy. Not that I liked to analyze every little thing—and I'd already decided I liked the way they talked in bed—but I also appreciated the fact that they talked at all. Doug had not talked in bed. I think once he told me "harder" or something like that, but he never looked at me or complimented me with either pretty words or coarse ones.

Excited and eager to hear more, my heart squeezed as I lay back and lifted my hips, and they wriggled my sweatpants off me. I was eager to feel more too. To come so many times I'd see stars.

"Nice socks." Lucas tugged one thick gray sock off, and I smiled. It was weird, but I felt just as desirable as they undressed me from sweats and socks as if I'd been wearing silk and lace. The warmth in their eyes as they studied me, the way their breathing increased, and the bulges at their crotches indicated that I affected them, even in my fugliest clothes, and that also made my heart contract.

And once more I lay naked between them. Ben ran a hand down the top of my thigh and his fingers lingered on the inside of my knee. My skin quivered at his touch. Lucas leaned in for a kiss on my mouth, slow and lingering, then he nibbled over my cheek and jaw, opening his mouth on my throat; his hands found my breasts and gently squeezed.

It all flooded back to me, the incredible sensation that had made me lose my mind. This was powerful stuff, the stuff that made people do crazy things, the search for pleasure like this. My eyes drifted shut, and I let them touch me everywhere, fingers tugging on nipples, mouths kissing, and tongues licking. I floated on a cloud of sensation, heat rushing through my veins. Hands measured my waist, explored my ribs, fondled my breasts, and my hips began to move with needy rhythm.

I opened my eyes to tell them they needed to take their clothes off, as I had last night, but I was too late. They were both already naked on the bed. Gorgeously naked. Ben's lean strength and dark-haired chest on one side of me, Lucas's bulkier muscles and smooth skin on the other. I reached out to touch, to feel their heat and strength. I found Ben's hip with my hand, and my eyes dropped to his erection.

I bit my lip, admiring his size and shape, then shifted my gaze to Lucas. My hand on his muscled thigh was so close to his cock, which was thick and hard, roped with veins. Despite their different bodies, their cocks were surprisingly similar in size and shape, both perfect and beautiful to my eyes.

Lucas groaned. "Fuck, Haylee. When you look at us like that, it makes me nearly lose it."

I blinked and lifted my eyes to his. "Like what?"

"Like you love what you see. Like you're starving for cock."

I swiped my tongue along my bottom lip. "I guess you can read my mind pretty well, then."

His eyes went dark, and Ben made a choking noise.

Power. I felt powerful. I did that to them, gave them enormous erections, made them want me. *Me.*

The part of me that wanted to hold up a hand and put a halt to everything and find out what the fuck was happening here gave way to the part of me that just wanted to go with it, and so that was what I did, intoxicated by my feminine power and surrender.

I leaned over and kissed Ben's mouth again, then turned to kiss Lucas. His tongue slid over my lips, and I closed my eyes, then felt myself moving as their hands lifted me and laid me down on my back. Once more I was the center of their attention as they stroked and kissed me everywhere, gently squeezing my breasts and pinching my nipples, until they both lowered their heads to my chest and each took a nipple into their mouth at the same time.

Sensation exploded inside me, zapping from their mouths to my core and then spreading outward through my entire body. My abs tightened on a hard shudder of delight at the incredible feeling of both nipples being sucked on—my newly discovered favorite thing. They drew my tender flesh into their mouths and pulled, hands cupping my breasts, and my back arched to push myself deeper. "Oh my *god*," I breathed. So much pleasure pooled in my pussy, a hard ache behind my clit, that I started pulsing. "Oh my god," I said again. "I think I could come . . . just from that . . ."

Without a word, Lucas slid a hand down my belly and between my thighs, the heel of his hand pressing against my clit, and that was enough to send me over. I came, hard, hips lifting, back arching, fractured cries falling from my lips.

My arms felt heavy, but I lifted them to lay my hands on the backs of their heads, still at my breast. As another tremor worked over my body, I dragged my eyes open and looked at them, my fingers in Ben's dark hair on my right and Lucas's caramel-brown hair on my left.

Ben's hand also slipped between my legs, over Lucas's, holding me there, and I pulsed into them. "Wow." He whispered it into my breast as he kissed the top curve. "Holy hell, Haylee."

"Nice alliteration." I heard two choked laughs and smiled lazily. "Sorry. Don't know where that came from."

"Great song hook," Lucas said. "Holy hell, Haylee, what have you done to us?"

"We are *not* writing a song about this. Holy bejeebus."

"Hmm."

They didn't stop touching me, continuing to nuzzle the curves of my breasts and cup my pussy, and I watched in fascination. Their faces were so close together above me. I traced a finger over Lucas's jaw, then a palm over Ben's hair.

Lucas's tongue blazed a trail up my chest. "Gotta be honest, Haylee. Wanna fuck you."

My pussy spasmed at the blunt words. I swallowed. "Yes. Both of you."

They looked at each other, another wordless exchange. Then they nodded.

I didn't just want that, I *needed* that, with a fierce, ravenous ache. Uncertainty about how it all worked spun away as they took charge, gently turning me over onto my stomach, hands once again caressing and setting my nerves alight.

Smooth strokes down my back delighted me, and then hands curved over my ass. Ben swept my hair aside and began to kiss me from my nape down my spine—hot, open-mouthed kisses—while Lucas's hands shaped the flesh of my butt, gently cupping and rubbing. His fingertips grazed the crease where ass met thigh, and I shivered. He drew his fingertips over the backs of my thighs, all the way to my knees and back up, and more shivers worked over my skin. And when I felt the graze of his stubbled cheek against the tender skin of my buttocks, I flinched hard. He rubbed his face there, lightly abrading me, then he too kissed me, open-mouthed, with tongue, right on the curve of my ass. His fingers played at the top of the crease between my cheeks where I was so sensitive, and I squirmed. "Oh wow," I whispered. My fingers curled into the duvet.

Once more they took their time, and it was remarkable. Lucas parted my thighs and lifted my hips, and I groaned into the bed covers at how exposed I was to him like that, my aching pussy bared to his gaze and his touch.

And touch he did; blunt, callused fingers slid up and down first over my sex lips, then between them where I was slick and wet. All the while his mouth moved over my ass, licking and nibbling, and when he sank his teeth into my flesh so gently, I twitched and gasped. Ben continued to stroke my back and kiss my shoulders and neck.

"Goddamn, you're so pretty," Lucas growled from behind me. And then, to my utter shock, he rubbed a wet thumb over my anus, eliciting waves of trembling pleasure. Again he licked and kissed and gently sucked on tender folds as he groaned with anticipation.

"Can't wait much longer." He moved his mouth away, his hands gripping my hips. "You ready, man?"

Ready for what? I tried to lift my head to look at Ben, and he gave my hair a gentle tug that sent more tremors cascading down my spine. My eyes met his, so dark and warm. He smiled at me. "Yeah, sweetheart. Up on your elbows, okay?"

He shifted on the bed so he was reclining against the headboard, pillows shoved behind his back. Between the two of them, they adjusted my position so I was right at Ben's groin where his beautiful cock rose up, flushed and gleaming at the tip. I licked my lips, and Ben moaned.

With a flash of delight, I got what they were planning. Lucas held my hips, nudging my knees farther apart with his, and then my eyes fell closed with pleasure as he began to stroke the firm head of his cock up and down through my sex. Slowly. Maddeningly. Up and down, between the cheeks of my ass, back down through the liquid center of me, rubbing over sensitive tissues.

"Oh that's nice," I moaned. "Oh my god."

I dragged air into my lungs and reached for Ben; he sucked in a sharp breath as I closed my fingers around him. He was thick and hot in my hand. I tried to focus as Lucas kept stroking me from behind. My lips parted as I studied Ben's cock—the defined ridge around the crown, the tiny slit, the pearly drop at the tip.

I deepened the curve in my back, pushing my butt up and giving Lucas better access, and tenderly cupped Ben's balls with my other hand. My elbows pushed into the mattress as my gaze wandered from Ben's groin to his thickly muscled thighs, dusted with dark hair, spread open on the bed. His body widened from narrow hips and waist to a broad chest and shoulders; his skin was dusky and smooth over lean muscle. He reached out and gathered my hair into a loose tail at the back of my head, and then I met his smoldering, dark eyes.

Heat zapped between us, and I felt like the air around us caught fire. My eyelids grew heavy as I stared at him, and he waited patiently, hands gentle in my hair. We both knew what I was going to do next.

Lucas's body bent over mine, his shaft still rubbing up and down against me, one hand sliding around under my belly until he was embracing me with that arm. His heat seeped into me, and I whimpered with the need that grew, desire multiplying into a relentless ache in my pussy.

"Please." I leaned my face closer to Ben. "Please. Fuck me. I need it."

CHAPTER 8
YOU MAKE ME BURN AND WANT TO FLY,

You make me smile and make me sigh.

Lucas groaned. "Oh hell, yeah."

And then I opened my mouth and closed my lips over the tip of Ben's cock, smooth and hot and delicious. I swirled my tongue around, eyes falling closed, delighting in the taste of him, the feel of him on my tongue, the stretch of my lips around his girth.

"Fuck yeah." Ben's fingers tightened in my hair. The tug on my scalp stung sweetly.

When Lucas moved away from me, my eyes opened wide and I turned my head, still keeping Ben in my mouth. What . . .?

But Lucas was rolling on a condom he'd pulled from somewhere —his jeans I presumed—and I sagged with relief. Yeah, that was a good idea.

And then finally, *finally*, Lucas probed at my hungry pussy, and pushed into me slowly. I couldn't stop the noises that rose in my throat. It might have sounded like I was in pain, and I sort of was, as Lucas stretched and filled me with a slight pinch and sting. He eased into me, inch by inch, sliding in and out in slow increments.

"Christ. Christ, Haylee, you feel so fucking good. So damn hot around my dick."

"Your mouth too," Ben added, his voice low and raspy. "Hot and wet. Suck me, baby, just like that."

Lucas growled, finally seated fully inside me, his hips pressed to my ass. "Goddamn." His hands gripped my waist and he went very still for a long moment. I felt him inside me, barely pulsing, filling me so deliciously. It was hard to concentrate on both men. I loved having Ben in my mouth, but I wanted to just pause and savor the feel of Lucas in my pussy. My body tightened and pleasure sharpened, and I craved that orgasmic release I felt hovering on the edges of my awareness. I needed to pay attention to that feeling, to reach for it . . . but I wanted to enjoy sucking on Ben too. I licked him up and down, wetting his beautiful shaft to ease its way deeper into my mouth, relaxing my throat to take him as far as I could.

He gasped, really pulling my hair. "Holy shit, Haylee. Fucking deep-throating me. Christ, that feels incredible."

"Oh man," Lucas groaned. "Seriously?"

"Oh yeah. Damn."

I wanted to smile, warmth spreading through me at their pleasure. Lucas began to move, long slow glides in and out of my pussy, torturing me. Pressure built, and Lucas linked his hands at my belly, easing me back against him as his thrusts deepened. My orgasm built faster than I wanted it to; I wanted to do this forever, but my mouth was tiring, and I had to release Ben with a gasp. I clasped him in my hands, my body jolting with Lucas's harder and harder strokes.

"So good," I moaned. "Oh my god. Lucas . . ."

"Yeah, babe? It's good?"

"Mmmm." I dropped my forehead to the mattress, between Ben's thighs. "Sorry, Ben . . . can't . . ."

"'S'okay, hon." His fingers gentled in my hair, stroking it back from my hot face, so tenderly.

Pleasure rushed at me, swelled inside me almost unbearably, and I pushed back into Lucas's thrusts. He slid his hand lower on my belly, then lower still to find my clit. Fingertips brushed across the sensitive flesh, slicked up moisture, then settled there to rub small circles. I cried out, my head lifted, and I got slammed by fiery sensation racing through me in hot pulses.

Lucas's hand went still on my clit, cupping me. "Fuck. Your pussy's so damn hungry, Haylee, tightening on me like that, Christ, it's making me lose it . . . Aw yeah, coming too, babe—"

And with a series of fast, hard pumps, his body slapping against mine, he came too, going rigid against my ass and then pulsing inside me. We stayed like that for long throbbing moments, then he laid a slow string of kisses up my spine.

I wanted to collapse onto the bed, but Ben was still unfulfilled, and I wanted to make him feel as good as Lucas and I did, so I pushed back up and took him in my mouth again. I brushed my fingertips over the soft skin of his testicles, then tentatively gave them a gentle squeeze, bringing forth a long, low groan from him.

"Oh honey." His hips moved, gently thrusting into my mouth, and I tightened my lips around him, squeezed the base of his cock with my hand and got lost in the rhythm of it. "So close. Oh yeah, so close . . ."

His balls grew tighter beneath his cock. I felt how close he was and quickened my strokes, and then he came too, his taste filling my mouth. I held him there, swallowing his essence, savoring him, loving the way his hands cupped my head with gentle firmness, loving his hoarse cries of pleasure.

When I opened my eyes, I saw Lucas's hand land on Ben's thigh and give a squeeze, and that touched something inside me. I licked my lips and swallowed once more, still tasting Ben, and then the three of us collapsed in a tangle of damp arms and legs. We all lay there, trying to catch our breath.

"Come here."

At Lucas's whispered words, I struggled to open my eyes, and found his face right near mine on the pillow. He curled his hand around the back of my neck and pulled me closer so our mouths met. His opened on mine, his lips firm and warm, and his tongue swept inside.

I still tasted Ben. And Lucas had to taste him too. His tongue rubbed mine, then licked over my lips. He gave a rumble in his chest, then crushed his mouth to mine again. The idea that he tasted Ben made my womb contract hard. I opened deeper for his kiss, and he sucked my tongue, so gently.

Then we drew apart and our eyes met. Lucas had a small notch of concern between his eyebrows, and he blinked at me. He touched his fingertips to my cheek, and his throat worked as he swallowed.

"You okay?" I whispered.

"Yeah." He paused, then said it again. "Yeah." He pulled me closer. Ben's arm came across my body, and in my heightened awareness, I knew his arm was over Lucas's body too. I closed my eyes and let lethargy sweep over me as I snuggled in between my two hot guys.

I awoke to the touch of hands on my skin, sliding over my waist and hips beneath the comforter of my bed, in the dark. Lips on my shoulder. Warm breath against the side of my neck. Fingers teasing a nipple into a hard, aching point.

I turned my face toward the lips nuzzling my hair. "Again?"

Ben murmured in my ear. "My turn." His fingers on my jaw turned my face to him and his mouth found mine in the dark.

I rolled to my side so we were pressed together from our chests

KELLY JAMIESON

to our knees. Behind me, Lucas's hand rubbed over my hip and thigh, and he kissed my upper back.

It was lovely and warm and decadent, and heat built inside me until I felt like my skin was burning. Ben's hand slid into my hair and held my head as he kissed me over and over, his sleek tongue rubbing against mine. I soaked up the sensation, awash with it, until I could let myself drift on it.

Hands turned and caressed me, and Ben moved over me. I lay on my back and reached for his big shoulders.

He used his knees to nudge my legs farther apart. "Oh yeah, honey." He slid his hands up my sides, all the way to my armpits, then pushed my arms up. Holding my hands in his over my head, he bent to kiss me again. "You're so fucking sweet."

I knew Lucas was still with us. I felt his substantial presence beside me, although this time he didn't kiss me. The bedroom was shadowy and dark but enough silvery moonlight came in the window that I could make out the angles and planes of Ben's face and body above me.

He moved his mouth from mine, kissing my jaw, my throat, and then the center of my chest. My breasts swelled in anticipation, and when he brushed his lips over a nipple, delight coursed through me. A moan rose in my throat, and I absorbed the helplessness of having my hands restrained above me while Ben rubbed his face over my breasts, dragged his tongue along an inner curve, then closed his lips over a tender tip.

My hips rose from the bed against his body. "Need you. Please."

"Yeah." He freed one of his hands, holding both my wrists in the other, and snaked his hand down between us. "You ready, honey? Oh yeah . . ." He gave a huff. "So wet."

"Dude. Here." Lucas's gruff voice penetrated the cloud of lust that surrounded us and as Ben's hand slid out from between my legs, I realized he was handing him a condom.

Ben paused, looking at Lucas. Another wordless exchange. The air around us thickened.

"I'm holding her hands," Ben said, in inexplicable obviousness. "Help me out here."

At first I thought Ben meant Lucas could help hold me down, which didn't seem necessary since I wasn't going anywhere. Then I realized he meant Lucas could help him out with the condom. I wasn't sure whether that seemed silly or hot. Either way, Lucas wasn't into it. He shook his head, eyebrows drawn together. Ben made a short noise that sounded like "shit" and released my hands to take the condom from Lucas.

Ben suited up quickly. I kept my arms up, bending my elbows a bit and sliding my hands beneath my head to lift it so I could watch him. The sight of his hands on his cock thrilled me—big hands with long fingers, his cock also big and so very hard. His fingers rolled on the latex with the same grace they played guitar, and a wave of delicious heat pulsed through me.

I'd never be able to watch him play guitar again without remembering this moment.

I'd deal with that later.

Right now, I just wanted that heavy cock inside me. My chest tightened and my breathing went shallow. I watched Ben hold himself, stroking the head through my wetness in long, slow glides. I tipped my hips even more, inviting him in, and he lifted his head.

In the shadows, his eyes met mine with a gleam, and his lips quirked. "Oh yeah. Lucas was right. Your pussy is greedy."

"I guess there's not much point in denying it." This elicited soft chuckles from both guys. "But what do you expect, when you do this to me? All this . . ."

Lucas stroked my hair back off my face. "We make you hot, huh, babe?"

"Oh yeah." I turned my head to kiss his hand.

KELLY JAMIESON

"Good." There was no mistaking the deep satisfaction that vibrated in the single word.

I was still drowsy and drunk on sensation, feeling like I was floating, and as Ben began to push into my body, I lifted to help him.

He gave another low laugh that turned into a groan as he eased into me little by little. "Fuck yeah. Hot and tight. Fucking killing me, Haylee."

My heart bumped and then expanded in my chest. Was it really me doing this to them? Making them feel so good, making them happy? It was like a dream, like it couldn't be real. I never wanted it to end, even though my body was rushing forward, tingling and heating, tension building in my womb almost unbearably.

Senseless from it, I let it consume me. My eyes fell closed, head back on the pillow, Lucas's hands stroking my hair and shoulders. Finally Ben was fully inside me, one arm sliding beneath my shoulders, the other tangling in my hair as his hips began to rock against me.

"Fuck. Fuck, this isn't going to take long. Sorry, Haylee, sorry. Want you to come—"

I wanted that too, but couldn't speak. I was very close, and just needed a bit more pressure . . . I shifted my hips once more, dug my heels into the mattress. There. Oh dear god, *there*. Ben's cock stroking inside me created a delicious friction that built and built, and then with his pelvis against my clit I began to convulse in hard, hot waves. My hands held on to his shoulders, the muscles dense and firm.

"Coming!" I gasped, my soft cries filling the room, and Ben's mouth turned in to the side of my neck.

His breathing harsh and ragged in my ear, his hips rocked faster and faster against me, fucking me into the mattress—and I loved it. I hooked my ankles around his back, wrapped my arms around his neck, and let him find his release. He went taut and motionless, a long, low groan ripped from his chest.

76

"Jesus fucking Christ. Fucking hell. Haylee."

Um, yeah. That was how I felt too. I stroked his damp, hot back and opened my mouth on his shoulder to kiss him, again and again.

"I hate fucking Christmas parties." It was the next night, and Ben, Lucas, and I had just arrived at Brandon's Green Hills home.

They each cast a sideways glance at me in the brightly light foyer of the mansion. "Yeah, babe, we get that." Lucas smiled as a gorgeous blonde in a skintight black dress took his jacket.

Ben wasn't quite so flirty with the coat check girl, and kept his focus on me. "Maybe someday you should tell us why that is."

Yeah, maybe not.

This was the second Christmas we'd been together, and I'd never explained to them why I dreaded the holiday season so much. The first Christmas, we hadn't been that close, and there hadn't been much need to explain. They'd gone home to spend the holiday with their families, and I'd been vague about my own plans. This Christmas was harder. They knew I wasn't close with my dad, and had each extended me invitations to go with them, which I'd politely declined. Then when Brandon had booked us for the gig at the Ryman, I hadn't been able to hide my horror. They'd been taken aback, and I'd quickly tried to cover up my dismay and brush it off, but now they knew I hated Christmas.

The blonde took my coat, and we moved into the house. The party filled every room on the main floor of the spacious, elegant house.

We greeted our host, obtained drinks from the bar, and began to mingle. I glanced at the humongous Christmas tree in the corner of the great room, all sparkling with white lights and covered with decorations, then turned my back on it to smile at Brandon. I kept that smile in place as I sipped my drink, a glass of wine that better suited the little black dress I was wearing than a beer.

Probably an hour passed. Lucas and Ben and I separated as we talked to other people. Christmas music played in the background, which made me clench my jaw, and my face hurt from the effort to smile. My feet were also hurting in the spiky black heels I was wearing. Tension climbed the back of my neck and tightened my scalp, and I knew I was going to have a headache before the night was over.

I managed to escape the great room with its big Christmas tree, but every room in the house had been decorated with glittery garlands and poinsettias and wreaths. In fact, there was a second tree in the more formal living room, just as lavishly decorated.

They were only symbols, and they didn't have to even mean anything. I kept telling myself that. They were pretty. I should be able to admire them just for the aesthetic pleasure of it. But they made my stomach tighten and my mouth go dry and then I had a flashback to that stage—all decorated with a similar glittery tree—and the Christmas song I'd been singing.

I had to close my eyes against it. It lasted only seconds, but it was enough to make my pulse rate spike; it felt like all the oxygen disappeared out of the room.

Oh for fuck's sake. Could I not even be in a room with Christmas decorations without this happening? I'd managed to avoid it for so many years, I'd really hoped I wasn't going to react like this. And yes, Christmas decorations are difficult to avoid, but I'd gotten very good at it over the years.

And anyway, it wasn't as if Brandon was going to make us pick up instruments and start singing for the crowd.

Feeling a tiny bit dizzy, I looked around for Ben and/or Lucas. I didn't want to embarrass myself by leaving the party early. If I did, they'd ask more questions. But if I was heading into a panic attack, I needed to get the hell out of there.

I excused myself from the group I was standing with and left the living room, wandered down the hall, peered into the great room, and spotted Ben on the far side of the room, near French doors that led outside. Fresh greens and twinkling white lights swagged the doors. He smiled down at a pretty brunette, his teeth white against his dark beard stubble, his smile so sexy.

I paused, my feet stuck to the floor as if someone had glued them there.

I blinked, watching him flirt with the girl.

I'd seen this a million times. I may have mentioned that Lucas and Ben have girls after them all the time? Well, it was no different tonight. And yet, it *was* different, because tonight I felt a stab in my heart.

Oh no no no. I pressed a hand to my chest. Just because we'd had sex didn't mean anything had changed between us. I'd never asked for any promises, and they hadn't offered them. And wasn't it enough without all that? The chance to experience—even if it was only temporary—the undivided attention of two men who made me feel feminine and sexier than I'd ever imagined possible?

So why did I find myself staring at Ben with another girl, feeling . . . Well, I didn't really want to analyze what I was feeling, because none of it was good, and it was better to just push that all aside.

My heart still tapped out a triple-time rhythm against my breastbone, though, which was somewhat uncomfortable.

And then things got even worse. When I turned to leave that room, I came face-to-face with Cheyenne Ranger.

It was a weird moment. We knew each other, but I didn't know if she knew that I'd been dating Doug. I mean, it was pretty common knowledge, but who knows what he'd told her, and I'd been away on the road for a while.

When her gaze skittered away from mine, though, I caught the flash in them and the faint color that washed into her face, and I knew that she knew, and I also knew that she knew *I* knew that she and Doug had been together. So it was altogether extremely uncomfortable.

My gaze went past her in case Doug was with her, and goddammit, he was. He was handing his jacket to the blonde at the front door.

Fucking hell.

The only way to avoid him was to duck back into the great room, where Ben and very possibly Lucas were otherwise occupied. Which meant I had to unstick my feet from the floor and face something I didn't want to see no matter what I did.

My heart rate accelerated even more, and breathing became difficult as my lungs refused to expand, the lack of oxygen making my head go even lighter.

I was not having fun at this party.

CHAPTER 9

IT'S ALL CHANGING, THERE IN OUR BED,

GROWING INTO SOMETHING MORE

"Hey, babe."

An arm slid around my waist, and I looked up to see Lucas flashing me a smile. He pulled me into him with a squeeze that felt so damn good.

"Um. Hey."

"Having fun?" The question was casual. Then his glance landed on Cheyenne. "Oh, hi, Cheyenne. Merry Christmas."

Cheyenne smiled, showing off her cute dimples. "Merry Christmas to you too. Both of you." Her gaze flicked to me and then back to Lucas. Doug approached from behind her, and I knew he'd seen me when his steps slowed.

Well, this was an awkward social moment. All I wanted to do was bury my face in Lucas's neck, but that wasn't appropriate. There'd been rumors before that we were a couple, and I certainly didn't want to add fuel to that gossip fire. On the other hand, maybe that was better than being the woman tossed aside by Doug Brandt for Cheyenne freakin' Ranger. Maybe a part of me wanted Doug to know I'd slept with Lucas, but the smart part of me knew I couldn't go there. It wasn't as if Lucas had never hugged me before. Doug probably wasn't going to think anything of the fact that Lucas had his arm around me.

It was amazing how many thoughts could pass through your head in a matter of seconds.

I fixed my eyes on Doug without smiling.

His eyes met mine, then shifted sideways. "Haylee. How was the tour?"

I lifted my eyebrows, aware of all the people around; a few of them were watching us. I tried to suck in a deep breath, fighting for control of my stupid body. Since my hands were shaking, I grabbed onto Lucas's arm where it circled my waist.

I did not want to let Doug off the hook, but I also didn't want to create a scene, because it would for sure be all over the internet and in the papers in the morning if I did.

"The tour was awesome." I tried to sound normal. I think my voice might have come out higher pitched than usual, but I could hardly hear myself over the buzzing in my ears.

Lucas bent his head and whispered to me, under the pretense of nuzzling my hair. "Got your back, babe. However you want to play this."

I leaned into him more and gave him a quick look of gratitude. His support suddenly made me feel stronger. I'd always known Lucas and Ben had my back, because we were a team, and we had been from the moment we'd banded together in our musical triad. That hadn't changed. Nobody else needed to know what had happened between us the last two nights. I knew. I knew I'd been a sex goddess. Okay that might be exaggerating. But still. I'd felt beautiful and desired. I'd felt powerful.

I lifted my chin and gave Doug a look, letting everything I felt for him show—my utter disdain for him, my contempt for how he'd treated me. I tossed my hair back and shook my head. "You're a douche bag, Doug." I leveled a look of pity on Cheyenne and patted her shoulder. "Sorry, hon. Things *don't* get better in bed." I smiled up at Lucas. "I could use another drink. How about you?"

He grinned. "Good idea. Later, guys." And we turned and headed to the bar.

Adrenaline zinged through my veins, and when we arrived at the bar, I had to lean on it to hold myself up. My legs had the strength of guitar strings. "Fuck."

"That was awesome." Lucas rubbed my back as he ordered another glass of wine for me and bourbon for himself.

"I'd rather have a beer." The room felt very hot.

"Want me to change that order?"

"Nah. It's okay." I sucked in air. "Shit."

"You did good, Haylee. The look you gave him—hell, he probably still feels that knife in his chest."

"You know what?" I turned sideways to face him. "I was freaked out at first. But I really don't give a shit. What kind of asshole would do that to a girl he's dating? Nobody worth my time, that's who."

"You are so right."

The bartender placed a glass of golden wine in front of me, and I picked it up and took a big slurp. I resisted the urge to wipe the back of my hand across my lips. When I looked at Lucas, his mouth was twitching.

"Slow down there, babe. Don't wanna carry you home like we did the other night."

A smile hovered on my own lips. "You did not carry me. I walked fine."

"Not quite."

"Okay, maybe I wobbled a little. It was the heels."

Our eyes met in a warm exchange. And held. My mouth curved up into a full smile, and I took another sip of my wine. Heat accumulated low in my belly.

Oh wow. I was just standing there smiling at Lucas and I was getting turned on.

Then I remembered Ben flirting with that girl, and my smile slipped. I looked down into my wine.

"What?" Lucas took my arm and shifted me away from the bar. "Why'd you suddenly look pissed off again? You still care about him, don't you?"

How could I tell him the real reason my mood had dipped? "No, I really don't. I just wasn't having a good time at this party before they even showed up." I rolled my eyes. "Too much Christmas. Christmas music. Christmas decorations. Christmas crap."

He studied me, and I shifted my feet. "You know we have to sing Christmas songs tomorrow night at the Ryman."

"I know." And I dreaded it. I knew every single one of the songs we chose. I hated every single one of them. But I could do it. It was "Opry at the Ryman," a great honor and opportunity.

I took another gulp of wine. Then Ben appeared.

"Hey, Haylee. Brace yourself, but Doug the slug is here."

I choked on my wine, nearly spraying both guys with it. "Doug the slug?"

He grinned. "Yeah."

"We already saw him," Lucas said. "And his lovely date."

"I called him a douche bag. I wish I'd called him Doug the slug."

"Feel free to use that." Ben's gaze searched my face as Lucas's had earlier. "You okay?"

"I'm fine." I hitched one shoulder. "He's a loser." I glanced around Ben. My insides tightened. I wanted to be as casual as I would have been a week ago about him flirting with another woman. "Who was that gorgeous brunette who was all over you?"

His forehead creased. "Who? Oh. You mean Nadine. She's a model."

"Of course she is."

He focused in on me. "Hmm. Jealous, sweetheart?"

I tossed my hair. I was getting good at that particular feminine gesture. "Certainly not. You can flirt with whatever girls you want."

They exchanged one of their looks: this time Lucas lifted one eyebrow at Ben, and Ben's look in return was cool enough to frost the short glass Lucas held.

I had no idea what they were communicating about, and this time I didn't care. "Actually, just before Doug the slug arrived, I was coming to find you to tell you I'm going home."

"Already?" They both said it and frowned.

"Just not my thing."

"Oh right." Lucas gestured toward the tree. "Too much Christmas crap."

They both gave me puzzled looks. I shrugged.

"Stay a little longer, Haylee." Lucas stroked my bare arm. "Then we'll all leave. Okay?"

"Just because I'm leaving doesn't mean you guys have to."

"Sure it does." He lowered his voice. "Because we're leaving *together*."

I knew what he meant. My knees wobbled and my wine sloshed up the side of the glass.

"You guys, this is crazy." Even whispering, I felt like everybody could hear us.

"Yeah. It kind of is."

"What would people think?"

"Why do people have to know?" Ben's matter-of-factness calmed my fluttery nerves. "They already know we live together."

I nodded, as his point had merit. *I* certainly wasn't going to tell anyone, and if people wondered—well, it wouldn't be the first time they'd wondered if there was something between Lucas and me. And even if there had been, it would be nobody's business but ours, and this was the same.

It was crazy, but it was *our* craziness. We weren't hurting anybody else.

Although I had a feeling somebody was going to get hurt. And that someone was probably going to be me.

With a smile firmly in place and a few more hair tosses, I managed to avoid Doug the slug and cute little Cheyenne as I schmoozed, and it was past midnight before I even realized what time it was.

As the car was taking us home, we passed the Gaylord Opryland Resort and the Grand Ole Opry on our left off the freeway, all lit up with twinkling white lights, and I had a fresh moment of doubt about the next night's show. A fist clutched inside my stomach, squeezing, as I thought about singing those Christmas songs in front of an audience for the first time since I was seventeen.

But once we were home, the guys started kissing me, and undressing me, and I let go of the tension that gripped me and lost myself in the heated, delicious focus of two men. Two men who'd had my back tonight, who'd been there for me, kept me going, and now gave me more pleasure than I'd ever known was possible.

The next afternoon, Ben and Lucas arrived home with a damn Christmas tree, much to my dismay.

"You guys!" I stared at it, hands on hips. "What is that?"

Lucas rolled his eyes. "Duh."

"Sorry, Haylee." Ben moved to set it up in the corner of the living room. "But it's Christmas."

"You guys aren't even going to be here for Christmas!"

"Come on. Help us decorate it. It'll be fun. We can listen to Garth Brooks's *Beyond the Season* album."

"No, thanks." I mumbled some bad words under my breath and disappeared into my room while they decorated it. I could hear them arguing about the lights being even and the tree crooked, and my stomach tightened. The way they were talking to each other scraped my nerves. It was more than their usual trash talking. Ben was short and uncommunicative, and Lucas was jabbing at him with unusual roughness.

Was the sex between us causing all this tension? But no—I'd noticed it even before we'd slept together that night in Sioux City. I didn't know what to do about it. As if I wasn't stressed enough about this concert, now I was worried about them too.

I got my stuff together for our gig at the Ryman, my insides cramping even more. When I emerged with my dress and makeup kit, they'd even hung up some lit garlands in the living room. I gritted my teeth and marched right past the decorations and out the door.

"Jesus," I heard Lucas mutter. "What's fucking *her* up?"

They didn't know. They didn't know I was about to do something I'd vowed I'd never do again. I was about to sing Christmas songs in public.

Although how I was going to get air into my lungs and relax my diaphragm enough to actually sing was a bit of a concern at that moment.

I'd agreed to this gig. I'd even rehearsed for it with the guys, and that had gone okay. We'd picked some songs, knocked together the arrangements between shows, run through them a time or two just to make sure. I hadn't enjoyed it, but somehow it hadn't been a problem singing Christmas carols before Thanksgiving even rolled around. It hadn't seemed real. Only now, in the season itself, and about to sing the songs in front of an audience, panic spiked inside me.

I was a professional. I could do this. It was an honor to be part of this evening. And I had my band to think of. I had Lucas and Ben to think of. I had to do this for them. They were counting on me to hold up my part of this deal.

The car service took us downtown to the Ryman. We got ready in one of the back stage dressing rooms and warmed up a bit, then stood in the wings listening to Brad Paisley sing "Santa Looked a

Lot Like Daddy," which made me glumly reflect how I'd never had that kind of experience. Every Christmas I'd traveled from bar to bar with my dad's band when all I really wanted to do was go home and hang a stocking on the fireplace and wait for Santa to come, like every other kid I knew. My parents had made me perform every night of the holidays, right until the New Year, dressed in red velvet and white lace ruffles, or sparkly sequined dresses that made me itch. I got Christmas day off from that, but even then I had to wear a fancy dress and sing for the family. After that last Christmas . . . I'd sworn, never again.

But here I was, about to sing Christmas songs, dressed in a sparkly dress. This time, though, the dress wasn't a problem. The dress actually made me feel . . . good. Sexy. Powerful. Maybe because when we went home, Ben and Lucas would strip me out of that red-sequined dress and make me feel beautiful.

You make me feel so beautiful . . .

Then, on stage, everything clicked for me. The lights, the applause . . . the music. The church pew seats were full of people, the atmosphere richly historic and intimate. And once again I followed Ben's advice and put all my emotion into my music. I put it all out there. I flirted with Ben and Lucas on stage. I flirted with the crowd. I pushed away the memories and focused on now.

Watching Lucas and Ben play guitar and sing tonight was turning me on. How weird was that? These were Christmas songs, for the love of cheese! The only really sexy one was our cover of "Santa Baby." I don't know why, but I got really into it, with some breathy "oohs" and shimmying dance moves around the chair Lucas sat on.

This was *so* not me. But dammit, I was having fun! The relief at being able to do this slid into something else . . . a relaxed calmness. A feeling of pure joy. Because of Lucas and Ben.

I surprised Lucas by slipping onto his lap, wrapping an arm around his neck and singing into his ear. When our eyes met, my stomach did a flip. He quirked the eyebrow and the opposite corner of his mouth lifted, and heat slid down through me. But I kept singing.

The crowd loved it.

Ben, however, did not seem to enjoy it so much. As the song ended, our last, I caught the way his head had dropped forward briefly, the corners of his mouth turned down. Of course he had a huge grin as he joined us to face the audience, but when I slid my arm around his waist as I often did on stage, his body was rigid.

What was that about? He didn't like my sexy little improv? I shot him a sideways glance, keeping my own smile firmly in place as the applause continued.

I'd watched Ben flirt with that girl at Brandon's party, and felt something like . . . jealousy. I'd told myself there was no reason to feel jealous. For one thing, Ben had come home with me, not her. For another thing, what was happening with us was just sex.

When the day came that both Lucas and Ben wanted to flirt with other girls and take them back to their hotel room and do dirty things with them, I'd deal with it then. It would be fine. I knew that, because I was always fine.

But Ben jealous of me and Lucas? That was crazy.

I still wasn't sure what was happening between the three of us. Things seemed to be getting more and more complicated.

We left the stage, Lucas as usual flying, Ben subdued, and me . . . confused.

It was the night before Christmas Eve and now that our gig at the Ryman was done, all the busy-ness was over. All the stuff that kept me from thinking too much about the fact that it was Christmas and I was going to be alone. Lucas and Ben were both leaving the next afternoon to fly home to be with their families for Christmas.

Maybe it would be good for us to all have time apart. It would be good for me to have some alone time, quiet time to write and read and listen to music. I could hang up a Christmas stocking like I'd always wanted to. Even though nobody would come to fill it with presents. Nah, that was a stupid idea. It would just be nice to have some downtime.

But weirdly, as much as that would usually appeal to me, I found myself contemplating the next few days with dread. Alone in a quiet, empty house didn't sound as nice as it usually did. God. I didn't want Ben and Lucas to leave.

That night in Lucas's big bed, I wanted to make things good between Ben and Lucas. I wanted to soften the rough edges between them, even though I didn't know what was causing them. I wanted to show Ben that he was an equal part of this and I cared about him too.

We lay on our sides, with Ben in front of me and Lucas behind, Ben kissing me while Lucas opened his mouth on my shoulder. Lucas pressed closer, his erection rubbing against my ass. Ben drew my knee up to his hip, then pushed his cock between my thighs, just as Lucas did the same from behind. Lucas went still against me, his fingers tight on my hip. The air around us went hot and electric. My belly did a roll of lust that turned into a slow melting feeling deep inside me.

"Relax," Ben murmured.

Was he talking to me . . . or to Lucas?

Lucas moved to roll away from me, but I reached a hand behind me to stop him. "No," I whispered over my shoulder, shocked at my own daring. "Don't leave. Want you here."

After a short pause, he shifted back against me, and this time it was me—god, I don't know where the boldness came from—who reached for his stiff prick and directed it back between my thighs. Sliding against Ben's cock.

I was acting purely on instinct. I didn't know if this was what they needed, or if this was going to make things worse between them. If it made things worse, they could blame me.

I felt the rumble of Ben's low groan.

And Lucas's sharp sigh against my hair.

Sandwiched between them, I felt safe, secure, and cared for.

Lucas's arm slid beneath me, curved around, and banded across my upper chest. His tongue blazed over my shoulder. His other hand roamed over my body, his hips moving against me in slow, sweet thrusts, and the air was so thick and hot it was difficult for me to breathe. My pussy ached unbearably. I needed them inside me. But I needed *both* of them.

"Relax." Ben's voice was low and husky. This time I knew he was talking to me because my body had stiffened. "It's okay, Haylee. It'll be okay. Right, Lucas?"

I wasn't so sure of that, but I wanted to go with it.

Lucas made a noise of agreement, his hips slowly rolling against me, his cock sliding along my pussy and Ben's cock. "Right."

Ben lowered his head to find one of my nipples with his mouth. He closed his lips around it and tugged gently. Oh dear god. Sensation rocketed through my body, fire licking through my veins. I felt myself get even wetter, and when Lucas moaned into my hair, I knew he too felt the increased lubrication on their thick rigid cocks. This was the sexiest thing I'd ever experienced. Holy, holy bejeebus.

I stroked Lucas's hip and thigh, rested my hand briefly there, then gripped his shoulder. The rhythm they'd found wasn't working quite right. It wasn't satisfying to any of us. I could tell, hot as it was. We needed to be closer. I tried to wriggle, but moving closer to one meant moving farther from the other.

Ben solved the problem by reaching over me and grabbing hold of Lucas, yanking him toward both of us.

Lucas grunted, but god, it was so good now. We were as close as we could be, the three of us rocking and rubbing against each other in a primal needy rhythm, all of us holding each other. Our bodies grew damp with sweat. Excitement rolled inside me. Friction on my clit started a buzz, a vague spiral of sensation. I needed more, so much more. "Please. Please."

Lucas rubbed his face against my hair. "Wanna be fucked, babe?"

"Yes." I managed to get the word out. "Yes. Both of you."

His lips touched my shoulder again. "Ever done anal, Haylee?"

A hard shudder worked through me. "No."

"You sure you wanna try that now?"

"No." I was honest. "I don't know what I want. I just need . . ."

"Yeah. We got it, sweetheart," Ben murmured. "Fuck, we need condoms."

"Got 'em." Lucas rolled away, then back, and passed one to Ben. "Right here."

I lay there trembling and panting while they gloved up. Then their hands moved on me, lifting my leg, shifting my hips. Lucas positioned himself behind me, pushing me against Ben's body as he entered me. Ben held me, kissed me, stroked hair off my sweat-dampened face.

Then Ben took his turn, sliding in and out of my body with delicious pressure as Lucas dragged his tongue down the groove of my spine. I let out a soft cry of pleasure.

They continued to take turns, increasing the pace until it was one thrust each, in and out, their cocks meeting at my pussy each time. If I could have taken them both at the same time, I would have, but I knew it was impossible.

This was amazing and hot and wicked, but there was no way I was going to come like this.

"Guys," I gasped. "I love this, but it's not gonna do it for me."

"Oh, babe." Lucas nipped at my bottom lip. "Let's fix that."

At that moment, I was ready to try anal. It scared the hell out of me, but I longed so much for them both, hated the idea that one of them would be left out after the way we'd started. I was ready to say the words I never in my life thought I would: *please fuck my ass!*

But they didn't.

Ben moved away, letting Lucas stay inside me. He nudged Lucas and me so that Lucas was almost on his back, taking me with him. Lucas lifted my top thigh, and in a haze of carnal delight, I watched Ben shift his body on the bed so his mouth was at my pussy. As his tongue came out and touched my clit, my body jolted with an electric shock. "God," I whispered, eyes closing.

Lucas cupped a breast while he began to slide in and out of me again in that beautiful rhythm. Ben's mouth teased me, his lips suckling gently on my pussy folds, his tongue tracing around my clit. Yes . . . oh god, yes, this was what I needed, this was so perfect, Lucas inside me, Ben licking my clit with wicked strokes. Sensations twisted together, coalescing into a hot throb that built hotter, tighter. It rose inside me with shocking intensity.

Ben licked lower. Through my hot erotic daze, I felt his tongue circling my flesh right where Lucas entered me, and realized it must be licking over Lucas's shaft as well. Lucas went taut behind me, his fingers tightening almost painfully on my thigh. He reared up from behind me to look at Ben. "What the fuck?"

Ben lifted his head from my pussy, leaving me throbbing into emptiness. I whimpered.

Ben gazed at Lucas, his lips wet, his breathing fast. Tension radiated off both of them as they stared at each other.

What? *What?* I was dazed, my vision blurry, my body buzzing with the need to come. "Don't stop. Please."

"Sorry, hon." Ben flashed his white teeth, then dipped his head again to lick me. His tongue flattened over my clit with exquisite pressure. Lucas began to move in me again—I swore he was harder than ever, thick and throbbing. He came so fast, groaning his release behind me, and when Ben sucked my clit into his mouth, I shot up and over too, fire streaking through me, burning me up, leaving me limp and breathless.

Ben's mouth had been on Lucas's cock. I almost thought I

could've imagined that, except for Lucas's reaction. I didn't know what to make of it. He'd seemed . . . shocked. But then he'd come so fast and so hard. He was still deep inside me. He gave a slow glide in and out, still hard, then he pulled out and rolled to his back.

Ben hadn't come. I peered at him where he reclined on the bed, his hand stroking his erection, wearing the condom. "Now you. Please, Ben."

I shifted my body so I was on my back beside Lucas, who let out a low groan.

"Think you can come again, hon?" Ben moved between my legs, hand on his cock.

"I'm not sure." My body was still tingling from the last orgasm. I watched him move over me. "But I'm willing to give it a shot."

Ben's smile glimmered as he stroked the head of his cock through my folds. "Atta girl."

Lucas rolled to his side to watch us. He caressed my breasts, my shoulder, turned my face to him for a kiss, then laid his palm on my abdomen as Ben pushed all the way into me.

My body tightened around him, squeezing on the fullness, the exquisite pressure. He held my thighs, his knees spread wide, and our gazes locked as he slid in and out in slow, lush strokes.

"Oh yeah." The tingle built, warm and buzzy, spreading through my body in bigger and bigger waves. Lucas slid his hand down my belly and found my clit. My body jolted when he touched me there, my hips rolling to meet Ben's deep thrusts.

Ben's eyes went heavy lidded. His lips parted. "Beautiful. So beautiful, Haylee."

I came again, this time slower and deeper, pleasure seeping all through my body. Ben gasped and groaned through his own release, his eyes closing, his hands gripping my thighs as he came in tight, pulsing jerks inside me.

I whispered my agreement. "Beautiful."

Much later, I lay there in the dark between two big, hot bodies, thinking about how they'd touched me, how many times they'd made me come, with tongues and lips, fingers, and cocks, how many times they'd come too. Heated memories of their cocks between my legs, touching each other, Ben's mouth on Lucas's cock, had me warm and aching.

That might also be something that should freak me out, but even though I had a million questions bouncing around in my head, it didn't. The three of us together had moved past the two of them and me. It had moved to the three of us as one sexual unit, and it felt only natural that they would touch each other too.

Was that what their other threesomes had been like? Honestly, I'd never thought about that. Not that I really liked to think much about them with another woman, but if I did, I figured those three-ways had been much like our first or second nights together. But perhaps not . . .

The idea of them touching each other in more ways than they had was so fucking hot, I think I nearly set the bed covers on fire. My body burned, and I slipped a hand down between my legs to where I ached. Again.

They clearly had feelings for each other. I mean, I'd always known that. But they were guys. They trash-talked and insulted each other. Lately that kidding around had taken on an edge: Lucas's banter harsher, Ben snapping in response or retreating into silence.

There'd always been a mutual respect and certainly some kind of caring beneath the trash talk.

They cared about me too. We'd been friends, close friends, the three of us.

But it was all changing, there in our ménage bed, growing and morphing into something that was still friendship but . . . more. Something that was sexual but . . . more. The dynamics and tempo were changing like a song moving from verse to chorus. I just wasn't sure how the song was going to end.

CHAPTER 10
LIKE A SONG MOVING FROM VERSE TO CHORUS,

Just don't know how the song's gonna end.

The next morning we slept late. When I eventually rolled out of bed naked, I did a full-body stretch with my arms above my head, then bent to pick up my panties from the floor where they'd landed last night. As I stood, I looked at the bed and saw both guys awake and watching me with hooded eyes and parted lips. Lust curled inside me, along with satisfaction that they liked what they saw. Only a week ago I would have been so self-conscious, but now I felt relaxed. Other than that tiny pinch because they were leaving for a week.

I slipped a big T-shirt over my head. "I'm gonna go for a run. Then I'll shower back in my own room. I know you guys need to finish packing and get to the airport." I resisted the urge to throw myself back into the bed and beg them not to leave.

In my room, I changed into leggings and a long-sleeved T-shirt, laced up my Nikes, and headed out. The weather was cool and over-cast, and I peered up at the sky dubiously. I hated running in the rain. The forecast hadn't called for precipitation, but the damp chill in the air told me it was likely. I'd only done about half a mile toward the golf course and the Cumberland River, along narrow, winding streets lined with sycamore and magnolia trees, when the drops started coming down, at first a few intermittent ones, then more and more.

Annoyed, I stopped, hands on my hips, and glared at the sky. More rain wet my face. Damn. I huffed out a frustrated breath, turned around, and headed back the way I'd come, toward home. By the time I got there, I was soaked and chilled.

I let myself into the house and took off my shoes so I didn't track water all over the hardwood floors. I padded down the hall in my sock feet, then stripped off my wet clothes in my bathroom, pausing before I stepped into my shower. Lucas's shower was amazing, a built-in tiled shower with multiple showerheads that poured water on you from every direction. The showerhead in the bathtub in my room worked, but after using Lucas's the last couple of days, I realized how much warmer his was. And I was freezing.

So I grabbed my robe and went back to Lucas's room where I'd left the guys a while ago. Hopefully Lucas wasn't using the shower or, if he was, he wouldn't mind if I used it too.

As I approached his room in my bare feet, I heard their voices, not yelling but definitely raised and terse.

Lucas was the loudest. "Or you could cut the bullshit and tell me what the fuck that was about!"

The bedroom door was still open as I'd left it, and I paused in the opening. With the blinds down and the afternoon light pale and gray with drizzle, the room was still dim and shadowy—but I could see Lucas standing beside the bed, naked and beautiful, his back to me. His hair stuck up all over the place as if he'd been running his hands through it.

Ben snapped back at him from the bed. "You know you liked it. For fuck's sake, would you get your head out of your ass."

I frowned and shrank back. They were fighting again, this time intensely enough that it scared me; the harsh tone of their voices made my skin tighten.

"Yeah, so you can put your *dick* in my ass. I know that's what you want."

Ben threw back the covers and stood, close to Lucas, getting right in his face. "Yeah. It is. And you fucking know you want it too."

"Fuck you." Lucas snarled and reached out to shove Ben's chest. Ben threw his arms up, knocking Lucas's hands away. My eyes flew open wide as Lucas drew back an arm as if to punch Ben. I covered my mouth with my hands and sucked in air, but they didn't hear me.

Ben blocked the punch, and they wrestled, fighting, trying to hit each other. Jesus! My heart began crashing against my breastbone. I wanted to yell at them to stop, but my vocal cords were paralyzed. Then Ben got hold of Lucas, flipped him to his back on the bed and fell on top of him. They glared at each other for what seemed like an hour, Ben stretched out over Lucas, both of them naked. It was Lucas who grabbed the back of Ben's neck and yanked him down toward him. Their mouths slammed together.

I slumped against the door frame as my legs turned into gummy worms.

They were kissing. A hard, long, brutal kiss, full of anger and undeniable passion.

Lucas made a rough sound in his throat. One hand still curled around Ben's neck, the other went to his shoulder. Thoughts swirled around in my head, unformed and incomplete. I thought Lucas was going to push Ben away. Or maybe hit him. "Fuck you," he muttered again when their mouths parted.

"I intend to."

Lucas groaned. "Christ. Oh Christ yeah, fuck me."

Oh my god, oh my god, oh my god. Heat rushed through me in

a powerful wave. I think I stopped breathing as I watched them; both of them remained oblivious to me.

Ben kissed Lucas again, and this time Lucas's arms wrapped around Ben's shoulders and his knees bent to allow Ben to settle between them. They both made low groans of pleasure.

My eyes widened, taking it all in, every detail. I'd approached quietly on bare feet so they clearly hadn't heard me. I took a step back, still in the door opening, but I couldn't drag my eyes away from them. I was so turned on I hurt, but I was also confused.

For a moment I wondered if I should join them—but what they were doing was so intimate and private and totally different than anything we'd done as a threesome, I believed they wouldn't want me there, that this was a moment for them and them alone.

I still didn't understand it and even though it was sexy and beautiful, it made my chest hurt so bad that a small noise escaped my throat. I took another step backward and out of the room, and then whirled and ran to my bedroom, trying to be quiet, but trying to get away as fast as I could before they noticed me there.

I carefully closed my bedroom door so it wouldn't make a noise, then stood leaning against it, eyes closed, heart thudding wildly. God. Oh god.

I moved blindly to the bed and my ass dropped onto it. I stared at the rug on the floor.

I'd thought it was hot that they'd touched each other. It felt natural when all three of us were in bed together. But now, seeing just the two of them, confusion filled me. Also fear.

I sorted through things in my mind, picking out some ideas and letting others go. I remembered things that had happened. I remembered the jokes they always made—like one time Ben had said something about how he was horny enough to do Lucas. I remembered Lucas kissing me after Ben had just come in my mouth, and I remembered thinking that he had to have tasted Ben too.

He'd wanted that.

They'd wanted each other all along. They just hadn't acted on it. Until today. I mean, it was possible that this *wasn't* the first time . . . but my gut told me it was. The way they'd been fighting . . . as if they were trying to resist it. That's what all the tension had been about.

Had all this been an excuse for *them* to get into bed together? Was *that* why they'd had threesomes before? So they could be together in bed and nobody would think anything of it?

Once again, I was the one nobody wanted. I was the tomboy, "one of the guys," the girl who'd rather watch football in her sweats than dress up in a skirt and makeup. They'd made me feel so good about myself, because they'd wanted me exactly as I was, without curls and makeup and sexy clothes, but in the end . . . they'd really wanted each other.

My fingers curled into my palms, every muscle in my body going rigid. Goddammit! Hot rage blew up in me, scorching pressure building.

They were having sex with each other just down the hall, without me. I couldn't deal with it. I couldn't face them. I had to get out of there. They'd leave for the airport in a while, I just had to get away for a few hours, and then I'd have the house to myself for the next week and by the time they came back, I'd have figured out what the hell to do about this.

With shaky hands I found dry clothes—a pair of yoga pants, a big hoodie. My damp hair was still in a ponytail, and I left it like that. My Nikes were wet but I shoved my feet back into them anyway and grabbed my purse.

As I left my bedroom, I ran smack into Lucas. He wore a pair of boxer briefs and a scowl. "Haylee. What the . . . Thought you went for a run."

"I . . . I . . . it was raining. I came back." My mouth felt dry and sticky, but my palms sweated. I couldn't meet his eyes.

He took hold of my upper arms to stop me. "What's wro—
Shit." His hands tightened on me. "You saw us. Didn't you?"

"Let me go." I tried to pull away.

"No, dammit. Wait." Lucas's jaw tensed and his mouth
compressed. His hair still stood in messy spikes.

I looked over his shoulder to see Ben, also bare-chested, his eyes
narrow, his mouth a grim line.

I sucked in a breath, lifted my chin, and straightened my shoulders. "It's okay, you guys. I get it."

Lucas frowned. "What do you get?"

I wasn't sure how to answer that. "You two . . . together. I get it. I saw
that. I've felt that for a while now." My voice rose and that swell of anger
rose up even hotter inside me. "And I get that you were using me."

Lucas's jaw slackened. Ben made a shocked noise.

My throat closed up embarrassingly, and I couldn't get words
out for a few seconds. "I didn't realize what was happening between
you two. But now I do."

"No, you fucking don't!" Lucas's shout made me shrink back.
"Using you? Are you fucking kidding me? Don't be such an idiot."

"Idiot?" I glared at him, heat sweeping from my hairline to my
toes. "Did you just call me an idiot? Well, fuck you. I'm done with
being used. My dad used me all my life, trying to make something
of himself. I'm *not* going to be used again. I'm *not* going to be
dumped again because I'm not good enough."

"What the . . . We weren't using you! Nothing happened! I
mean, I couldn't do anything. With him."

Ben made a noise and my gaze flicked to his face, drawn into
tight lines of despair.

I refocused on Lucas. "I saw you kiss Ben! I heard you ask him
to fuck you."

His jaw tightened. "Yeah. I asked him to. I wanted it. But when
it came to actually doing it . . . I couldn't . . ."

"Jesus fucking Christ." Ben scrubbed a hand over his face. "You are such an asshole."

My mind was leaping all over the place trying to make sense of this. Lucas was attracted to Ben, but in denial about his sexuality? Was that what this was?

"Fuck." Lucas turned his glare on Ben.

Ben scowled back at him. "What is your problem? You wanted it too, you know you fucking well did."

I stared in horror at the scene unfolding in front of me.

I wrenched my arm away from Lucas's grip. "I need to leave. You guys go . . . do whatever you want. Go home and do your Christmas stuff . . . When you get back, I'll be gone."

I shoved out through the front door, their curses ringing in my ears. They both followed me, but they weren't even dressed and it was pouring rain, so they didn't get far. I ran to my car and jumped into it, shoving the key blindly into the ignition.

I started driving. I didn't know where to go; I was mindless, thoughts spinning. McGavock Pike was narrow here, with no shoulder and a steep drop off the side, and when my wheels hit the edge of the pavement, my heart lurched. I shouldn't be driving like this. Where could I go? It was Christmas Eve. My other friends were busy with family stuff. Opry Mills mall would be insane.

I pulled into the parking lot of a restaurant on the other side of Briley Parkway. Inside, seated in a booth next to the window, I ordered a hot chocolate and a donut with red and green sprinkles that almost made me throw up when I tried to eat it. Not that it was bad. It was just that I was sick with worry and fear, and my throat closed up when I tried to swallow the sweet pastry. I sipped my coffee and leaned into the wall. Brooks and Dunn sang "Winter Wonderland" in the background.

I sat there for a long time, watching the rain stop and the sky clear somewhat, just as the sun began to lower in the sky. I thought about what I'd seen. I thought about Ben and Lucas having sex together without me. Questions formed to which I had no answers.

Had this ever happened before? Were they gay? Were they in love? How could I not know that if it was true? Was I a blind idiot?

I was pretty sure nobody could be that blind. Which meant this was the first time it had ever happened.

The country music biz wasn't exactly known for being welcoming to gays, but I did know some people who were openly gay. There weren't many big stars who were out, but common sense said there had to be more. There were rumors. Probably some based on truth. I didn't care. Someone's sexual orientation was a nonissue with me.

But it fucking *burned* that they'd used me to be together.

I became aware of the looks I was getting from the few people working in the restaurant. I was the only one left there, and they were getting ready to close. I blinked at the gathering darkness outside the windows.

It was probably safe to go home now. Ben and Lucas would have left for the airport. In fact, they were probably already on their flights.

The home that used to feel like a sanctuary, a haven from the real world, a place I could be alone or hang out with my two favorite people in the world, a place where we made magic and created music—and most recently had hot, dirty sex—now seemed scary.

How could I ever go back there?

I slipped on my jacket and gathered up my purse, leaving the donut with one missing bite on the table, and walked out. The air outside felt lovely and fresh after the rain.

I started driving, thinking I should go home, but I turned right instead of left, then turned left again and somehow found myself at the Gaylord Opryland Resort. Decorated for Christmas, it sparkled with thousands of white lights in the trees. The wet pavement reflected the lights back in a shimmery glow that intensified the glitter and glitz. It was so overwhelmingly Christmasy it made everything inside me ache.

The gazillions of sparkling lights drew me against my will. I ended up parking my car in the lot of the mall and walking up to the Grand Ole Opry. A big tree all decorated and sparkly sat on the plaza in front of the building, and more white lights twinkled in the trees all around. I took a seat on the curved stone bench facing the Opry and gazed at it.

I remembered when I was sixteen years old, my parents brought me to Nashville. It was just before mom died of cancer. We knew she was in the final stages. She and Dad wanted to see Nashville before she was gone, so we'd done that bittersweet family trip. We visited the Grand Ole Opry, which was like a shrine to my dad. He'd always dreamed of playing there one day.

Mom had been all happy and smiling, so optimistic that one day Dad and I would be there singing on the stage at the Grand Ole Opry. Mom was dying. So we all went along with that.

But even at sixteen, I'd known Dad would never play there. He had some talent, yeah, but not enough to ever get as far as he'd wanted to go. Even then, I understood that he'd pinned all his hopes on me, and at that age I wasn't so sure I would ever make it there either.

After Mom had died, it had become even less likely Dad would ever make it that big, because he'd drowned his sorrows in a whiskey river, as Willie would say. God. I closed my eyes, thinking about how life had deteriorated after her death. Tears stung the corners of my eyes as I waited for that familiar twinge of guilt, and yup, there it was. I'd abandoned my poor old dad to pursue my own dreams, leaving him all alone in Grand Forks, playing guitar and singing when he wasn't too drunk to string some lyrics and chords together. I'd headed for the big city of Los Angeles, without him and without the country music I'd tried to reject.

But here I was, in front of the Grand Ole Opry. It had been Dad's dream, but I'd made it there. I'd played at the Grand Ole Opry. With Ben and Lucas. My parents hadn't been there to see it— Mom was gone and my dad was still angry at me for leaving, too bitter to be happy about my success. And now my heart pinched at the thought that I'd thrown all that success away—because I'd wanted to know what a threesome was like.

I was lying to myself, of course. There was much more to it than wanting to know what a threesome was like. I'd wanted to sleep with Ben and Lucas. Both of them. I cared about them both. I couldn't imagine being without either of them. It was fucked up, but it was how I felt. And now I had neither of them.

They wanted each other.

My stomach churned, and I pressed a fist against my abdomen. Could we salvage something from this? Could we stay together as a group?

I pictured myself with them, writing, singing, performing. Pretending I was happy so they wouldn't feel bad. Me, living alone. I could do it. Sure I could.

No, I couldn't.

Not only had I thrown away career success, I'd lost the two men I loved. The pain almost doubled me over. Surrounded by twinkling lights and Christmas music, I had never felt so alone in my life.

Time to go home.

Back at our house—which, as I expected, was empty and dark— I took off my jacket and still-damp shoes. I changed my socks for big thick gray ones and wandered out to the kitchen. Meh. I had no interest in food. I trudged into the living room. I stood there in the dark for a moment, and then I moved to the plug for the Christmas tree Ben and Lucas had insisted on putting up. It glowed to life, the lights twinkling red, green, and gold, sparkling off the ornaments. With a sigh, I plugged in another cord, and the white lights in the garland swagging the fireplace and French doors also lit up.

It wasn't lit up like the Gaylord Opryland Resort, but it pushed back the blackness and added a little light and warmth to my dark night. I stared at the tree, remembering listening to Ben and Lucas bicker as they'd decorated it, Lucas trying to give orders, Ben complaining that Lucas had no taste at all. And me, trying to hide in my room, worried about the way they were snapping at each other, the increasing tension between them, while trying to deal with my own Christmas demons.

I'd thought I wanted to be alone at Christmas. I'd convinced myself and the guys that I was looking forward to it. And now I knew that was really the *last* thing I wanted. My chest ached with a pressure that rose up into my throat.

I turned on the torchiere lamp in the corner of the room, and it shone up to the ceiling. In the indirect illumination, my gaze fell on my piano, my beloved baby grand. I drifted over to it and sat in front of the keys, my hands resting lightly there. I closed my eyes and tipped my head back, and my song filled my head again.

I'm lost, aching and longing for something I can't have.
Pleasure like this makes people do crazy things.
You make me lose my mind.
Part of me wants to stop,
Part of me wants to go,
Part of me wants to know
Because I don't know how to do this.

I almost fell off the stool when a deeper voice joined in with me on the last line, singing perfect harmony.

My head jerked up, and I saw Lucas standing in the shadows just outside the glow cast by the lamp.

CHAPTER 11
CAN'T STOP MYSELF FROM CARING,
EVEN THOUGH MY HEART STILL HURTS.

I stared at Lucas.

He continued singing in his bass voice, "Gonna show you how to do this. Gonna show you how to fly. Gonna make you smile and make you sigh. Gonna make you want things you've never had and fill you up with wanting more."

And together we sang, "More love."

Our voices faded into silence. Emotion rushed in and filled me up, twisting me inside out.

"Where the fuck were you?" Lucas advanced on me. "Fuck, we were worried sick about you."

He stepped closer, shoulders hunched, hands in the pockets of his jeans. My gaze shifted behind him, but I didn't see Ben. I stared at him. "Why are you still here?"

"You fucking think we were going to leave after that? Where the hell did you go? Jesus fuck, we were worried."

"Y-you didn't catch your flight?" I shook my head, confusion filling me.

He crossed his arms. "Fuck no."

"Where were you?"

"Out looking for you. Are you okay?" The intensity in Lucas's eyes, the relief, the concern, made me blink.

"I'm fine," I lied. "Um, where's Ben?"

Lucas scowled. "Fuck if I know." He rubbed his face. "He was pissed. He left right after you did."

"He didn't go home either?"

"I don't know. Don't think so."

"Oh god."

"I tried to call you, but your cell phone was in your room."

"Oh. Yeah." My cell phone had been the last thing I'd been thinking of when I'd torn out of the house. "What about Christmas with your families?"

Lucas slashed a hand through the air. "We'll see them some other time. We need to talk."

My stomach tightened, and I closed my eyes briefly at the wave of sickness that swept over me. I didn't want to have this conversation, but he was right. "Yeah. I guess we do." I swallowed through my tight throat. "Tell me what happened. With you and Ben, this morning."

He gave a jerky nod. "After you left to go for your run, we went back to sleep. When I woke up, we were . . . touching. I got out of bed, and we started to argue. I was pissed off about what he did last night . . . well, pissed off and turned on."

It was freaking me out to see Lucas, so confident and assured and in charge all the time, stumbling and looking lost and confused. I wanted to comfort him. Yeah . . . I couldn't stop myself from caring, even though my heart still hurt. "I saw that," I whispered. "I saw you guys arguing. Fighting. I thought you were going to punch each other."

"I tried." A smile flickered over his lips. "But I couldn't do it. I told him that. I was trying to explain why, but he . . . he didn't understand what I was trying to say. I . . . I hurt him."

Oh my god. Oh my god. Sharp splinters of heat burst in my

chest. I ached to think that Ben was hurting, that he felt rejected by Lucas when he obviously had feelings for him. Because I cared about Ben too.

What a fucking rat's nest of a mess this was. How could love be so fucking complicated and painful? I sucked in a shaky breath. "Do you love him?"

"I . . . I care about him. I'm confused. It's hard to accept that my sexuality is so . . . fluid."

I nodded and bent my head. He loved Ben. I knew it. Anguish squeezed my lungs and my eyes burned. "It's okay. Don't worry. I'm leaving. And you two can be together."

"What?"

I nodded, my throat closing up, but I managed to shape my mouth into a smile that I hoped looked reassuring.

"Sing the end again," he instructed me gruffly.

I blinked. "What?"

"The end of the song. Sing it."

"I don't want to."

This song was too personal, too revealing, especially in the face of what had happened.

"Haylee."

He'd already heard it once, when I didn't know he was there. Slowly I shifted again on the stool. My fingers found the keys, and I sang the words again accompanied by soft chords.

Drowsy and drunk, feel like I'm floating,

Can't stop myself from caring, even though my heart still hurts.

Then Lucas sang the chorus with me, and his voice made goose bumps rise on my skin as he sang the last lines:

You make me want things I've never had and fill me up with wanting more—

More love.

When I finished, Lucas kept singing, sharing the part he'd had in his head the other day.

I listened to him without looking at him, letting the words seep into my consciousness.

Can't believe you love me too

And it's not wrong because we should never be ashamed of love.

What did they mean? Was he being as honest and raw as I was? Who was he singing them to? Ben?

I lifted my head to look at him, and our eyes met across the short distance separating us.

"This is so fucked up," he muttered. "I said it's hard to accept that I could care about another man that way. But it's even harder to accept that I could be in love *with two people.*"

My heart stopped beating. My breathing suspended. My head went light. "What?"

A million questions backed up in my brain. I thought I'd figured it all out, but he was messing with my mind now.

He came closer and to my shock, he went to his knees on the floor in front of me. He slid my butt around on the stool so I faced him. "I have to tell you this. Everything's gotten all fucked up. I don't know what to do. But I have to tell you. I love you. I've loved you forever." His eyes closed then, lines of agony drawing his brows together and turning down the corners of his mouth.

He loved me. Oh god, he loved me. But . . . "But . . . Ben—?"

He opened his eyes and met mine. "I love you," he repeated, confusing me even more. "But I . . . I apparently have feelings for Ben too. But Christ, he was so pissed off when he left. I know he thought I was rejecting him, that I was denying how I felt for him."

I held his gaze. "Weren't you?"

"No!" He squeezed his eyes shut, his face contorted into lines of misery. He pulled me off the piano stool and onto his lap, wrapping his arms around me, his body vibrating with emotion. "Christ, I fucked up."

I had to touch Lucas. Confusion swirled inside me, but I lifted my hand and pressed my palm to his cheek.

I loved Lucas. And Ben. Lucas loved me. And Ben. Ben . . . loved Lucas. My heart squeezed. What was the solution to this fucking mess? *Was* there a solution? How on earth could we stay together and make music after all this?

My body felt heavy and tired and achy. It was too much for me to deal with.

I pressed my face into Lucas's neck. "I want to get drunk."

I felt his body shake, and I pulled back to see that he was laughing. His silent laugh turned into a groan as he pulled my head back to his shoulder. "Yeah. Me too."

But neither of us moved to get up. We sat on the hardwood floor in the dining room, next to my piano in the silent house, which was dark other than the floor lamp in here and the twinkling Christmas lights in the living room. I was grateful that I wasn't alone, but sad that Lucas wasn't home with his family for Christmas, and worried about where Ben was.

Merry effing Christmas.

And then the *beep-beep-beep* of the alarm system broke the quiet as a door opened. Both our heads jerked up. The front door shut and quiet footsteps slapped on the hardwood floor. Ben walked into the living room, looked around, and then spotted us on the floor through the French doors. He stopped.

We all went statue still. Ben took in our position. I couldn't see his face in the dark.

Lucas and I looked from Ben to one another. Now it was our turn to share one of those wordless glances.

Ben spoke first, his voice uneven. "I see you found her."

"Yeah."

"You okay, Haylee?"

"Um. I'm not really sure."

"Thanks for letting me know she's okay." Ben gave Lucas a glare laced with bitterness.

Lucas sighed. "I just got home myself."

Lucas and I let go of each other, and I slid off Lucas's lap and rose to my feet. Lucas stood at the same time, reaching out a hand to help me. He slid an arm around my waist.

Ben's gaze dropped to where Lucas embraced me. "You two have apparently talked."

"Yeah."

"You want me to leave? I mean leave the house. Leave the group. Fuck." Ben rubbed his eyes. "I shouldn't have come back."

My heart was pounding wildly. "No, Ben. Don't go. We all need to talk. And maybe *I'm* the one who'll be leaving."

"No." They said it in unison. Lucas's voice was sharp, and his hand tightened on my hip.

My eyes flew to Ben's face. We stared at each other.

"Haylee." He let out a long exhalation.

Lucas's fingers dug into my side. "Earlier. I told you I heard her. She got the wrong idea. And so did you."

"Well, fucking explain it to me, then!" Ben's hands curled into fists. "Tell me why your tongue was down my throat one minute and the next you were shoving me away like I repulsed you!"

I turned my gaze to Lucas. I wanted to know the answer to that too.

"Shit." Lucas scrubbed a hand over his face. "I was going to explain it to you, but you got all pissed off."

"Explain it now!"

Tension vibrated around us, and my stomach knotted up. I divided a look between them and sank my teeth into my bottom lip.

Lucas sucked in a breath. "I only pushed you away because I wanted Haylee to be there too." He focused on me. "I wanted it, but I couldn't do it without you there. I felt like it was cheating on you."

I blinked at him. I tried to breathe, but my lungs felt burning hot. "Cheating on me?"

"Yeah. I know it's crazy. I don't get it either, believe me. I just . . . I've wanted you for so long, Haylee. And then I finally had you . . .

with Ben. I can't tell you how fucking amazing that was. Finally. I was with you. I was going for it, pushing you to do it again. And again. And then I realized . . ." He turned his gaze toward Ben. "I want you too, Ben. But I couldn't do it. It felt like there needed to be all three of us there. I was trying to tell you that, but you didn't get it. I mean, I guess I didn't explain it very well. God help me, I love you both. I need you both. I needed you both to be there for that."

"Fuck," Ben breathed. "Seriously?"

Lucas nodded.

Ben's eyes closed. "I thought you were rejecting me." I could barely hear Ben's low, rough tone. "Because—because you didn't want me. I thought I fucked everything up. By telling you how I felt about you. I was so pissed off at you. I could tell you wanted me too, and you were fucking denying it, pushing me away." He shook his head. "I always screw up anything good that happens to me, but this was the worst."

"I'm sorry." The raw agony in Lucas's voice made my heart hurt. "You didn't screw up, I did. You were pissed, then Haylee was pissed, and I thought I was the one who fucked it all up."

I couldn't stop the shocking laughter that bubbled up. They both blinked at me. "And I thought it was all *my* fault."

Reluctant smiles tugged their lips.

"I thought I never should have asked you guys for a threesome. That just screwed everything up. This would never have all exploded in our faces if it weren't for that."

We would have continued keeping our feelings for each other locked deep inside us, so deep we didn't even recognize them ourselves.

Lucas stroked my hair again. "See, that's why it was a *good* thing. It was all building up. It was going to explode in our faces at some point anyway. We needed to figure out how we all really felt." He lifted his chin to look at Ben again and extended one arm. "Come here."

I waited, still gripping Lucas, my front pressed to his side, my arms around him. His body was as tense as mine.

I looked at Ben. I loved him so much. Was he processing the fact that Lucas loved me too? How did that make him feel? I didn't want to hurt him. Would it make a difference if he knew I loved him too? Did I have the guts to tell him how I felt? He was sensitive and empathetic—I could imagine him being upset about hurting me because I loved him and he loved someone else. The words clogged up inside me and my stomach twisted painfully.

God, I'd loved these guys for so long. I squeezed my eyes shut and once again tightened my arms around Lucas's waist. How could I live without them? Without both of them?

I could live. I *would* live without them, if I had to. Because it seemed likely that was what was going to happen. Three people didn't have a relationship. And if they did . . . well, that was all kinds of fucked up and complicated and holy hobbling Christ on a crutch, what would people say about that? It was too crazy to contemplate and besides . . . I had no idea if the guys wanted something like that.

But if nothing else, I'd learned that we needed to be honest with each other. Keeping our feelings locked down inside us hadn't been a good thing.

"Ben. Please. Come here." I could barely swallow, my throat was so rigid. I too extended a hand to him. "I'm in love with you too."

Emotions flickered on his face—his eyebrows rose, then lowered, his mouth tightened, his eyes flashed. "What?"

"I love you." I held on to Lucas for dear life as I repeated it. "I love both of you. And Lucas feels the same."

"I was trying to tell you, man," Lucas said. "I'm still all fucked up about this. I've been in love with Haylee forever. I was in denial that I had feelings for you too."

Ben's eyes narrowed and he watched us, his posture stiff.

My eyes stung. "You don't believe us."

His head jerked.

"I know you don't feel that way about me," I rushed on, "which is why I said I'll be the one to leave. But——"

"No." Ben shook his head. "You're not leaving. I don't want to lose you."

Waves of electricity pulsed around us in the room.

"I don't want to lose either of you," he continued. "I thought—wait, is this for real? Because I'm losing my shit here."

"It's for real." Lucas's voice roughened.

Ben started walking toward us. "I was so worried about you, Haylee. You looked so hurt when you ran out of here. I was hurting too, and furious at Lucas. And at myself. I was afraid I'd wrecked everything."

CHAPTER 12
WE KEPT OUR FEELINGS LOCKED DEEP INSIDE,
SO DEEP WE DIDN'T EVEN KNOW THEM.

My chest had gone tight, my lungs burning as I tried to breathe. "Ben," I whispered.

"I love you too, Hayley," Ben continued, his voice cracking. "You gotta know that."

My eyes widened and my heart exploded into a rapid beat. "But—"

"It's crazy." Ben was now close enough to touch. "Totally fucking nuts. I don't get it. At all. But there it is. I love you both. I have for so long. And I can't fucking believe you feel the same."

I reached out to Ben. Lucas did the same with the arm that wasn't around me. Ben moved into us. We stood there, foreheads together, arms around each other. Silence expanded in the room, only the sounds of our uneven breathing reaching my ears above the pounding of my heartbeat. I closed my eyes.

Emotion swelled up in me, huge and terrifying. Was this really happening? Ben wasn't wrong—it was crazy. Insane. But unimaginable happiness was stealing through me, even though I was afraid to let it.

After a moment, I pulled my focus away from myself and thought about my two guys. I still had more questions.

"After that first night," I said, looking at Ben. "In Sioux City. It seemed like you regretted what had happened. Like you didn't want to do it again."

He huffed out a laugh. "Right. Christ." He closed his eyes briefly. "I wanted it so much. But fuck, I was terrified." He opened his eyes. "I watched you two together on stage. The last night in Sioux City—the chemistry you had. Everyone saw it. At the Ryman . . . You look great together. Everyone's always talked about you two being a couple. I started to think that's where that was going."

"Oh god," I whispered. I set a palm on his face and stared into his eyes. "No. No, no, no."

"Fuck," Lucas muttered, his hand tightening on Ben's shoulder. "Ben . . . sorry. I was struggling too. But I'm so fucking sorry."

I nodded. "Ben . . . are you gay?"

He shrugged. "I've always been attracted to guys and girls. Since I've been in Nashville, I tried not to look at guys. Figured things would go better if I just acted straight. It wasn't hard. Musicians have girls chasing after them all the time. Sexy girls. I had no problem being with them. Until you guys both moved in here." He looked at Lucas. "Fucking hell, it was hard to pretend I didn't want you." He closed his eyes and tipped his head back. "It was getting harder and harder."

I nodded. I'd felt it too. I just hadn't exactly realized what was causing all the tension. "Why . . . why don't you do relationships?" I'd always wondered about this, always assumed he'd been hurt somehow.

"Never felt right," he said. "When I was with a girl, I just felt like . . . I had room for more. Same thing when I was with a guy. I gave up on ever finding the one who'd feel right. Never felt like I could open up about what I really wanted, or tell them I had room in my mind and heart for them, but also for *more*. Figured I was just meant to screw around forever. Then I met you. Both of you. I was falling for both of you."

"Oh, Ben." I squeezed his waist.

"Being around you all the time. Haylee . . . you get me." He stroked a hand over my hair. "You're so funny and sweet, and unassuming. You have no idea how gorgeous you are. And you're never sexier than when you're singing. I've been burning up inside over both of you, scared shitless that I was gonna screw things up and destroy everything we've worked for. And then . . . I did."

"No," Lucas said roughly. "You didn't screw up. We're gonna work this out."

I closed my eyes and sucked in a deep breath. "You weren't using me."

I opened my eyes to see Lucas scowling at me. "Fuck no. I was furious when you said that."

"How could you think that, Haylee?" Ben touched my jaw.

I shook my head. "Be-because it's happened before. You guys know my story. How my dad used me. How guys always thought I was just a buddy. You made me feel so beautiful, but I let my own stupid insecurities get to me. I let you down because I didn't trust you or believe that you could both want me. Then you were fighting and angry with each other and I walked out on you when you tried to explain things and everything was fucked up. I thought I'd lost you, I thought I'd lost *everything* because I'm so messed up." I swallowed and met their eyes, first Ben's, then Lucas's. "I'm so, so sorry."

"Haylee." Ben leaned his forehead against mine. "Believe in yourself."

I nodded, my chest full of emotion.

And now I stepped outside myself, realizing how important this was for them. For Ben—who'd loved Lucas for a while now, probably despairing of ever having that love returned—and Lucas, who'd only just been able to admit his feelings for a man he'd seen as a friend and bandmate. This had to be even bigger for them than it was for me. Although for me it was pretty fucking huge. I felt a need to help them, to make this go well for them.

"I love you guys. I want you to be together."

They both stared at me, and when Ben's eyes narrowed and Lucas's forehead creased, I realized they didn't get what I was doing.

"I'll be there with you. All of us. Together. But I want you to be together."

Their expressions cleared. Ben's eyes darkened, Lucas's eyes flickered. I could tell he was still unsure about this. And who could blame him? I suspected he'd never been with a man before, but this wasn't the time to discuss that. This was the time to cement this relationship between the three of us.

I gave them a look—a chin-lifted, go-ahead-and-do-it look. They turned to each other.

"Christ," Ben groaned, and he lifted a hand and slid it around the back of Lucas's neck. He brought Lucas's face closer and their eyes met. I watched the sizzling exchange, watched Lucas's long eyelashes flutter as he studied Ben's face, watched Ben's lips part in anticipation.

And then they kissed. Fierce and hard and achingly beautiful, their mouths joined and open to each other, eyes closed. My heart clenched. My pussy ached. I clasped my hands together in front of me and watched them.

They broke apart, breathing hard, and leaned their foreheads together.

"I don't do relationships." Ben's hand closed over Lucas's shoulder.

Lucas snorted. "Yeah? Well, I don't do men. Get over it."

We all chuckled.

"Fuck," Ben muttered.

"Yeah," Lucas said, the corners of his mouth twitching. "Let's do that."

Their heads both turned, and they fixed their gazes on me. I smiled. "Yeah. Let's do that."

My insides were jumping. I hurt with need, and I knew I was wet. Lucas took my hand and then Ben's, back in charge, and led us down the hall.

In the dim quiet room, Lucas released our hands and turned to face us. The air around us pulsed with anticipation and emotion. Lucas touched my cheek and bent to kiss my mouth, then set his other hand on Ben's shoulder, edging him closer. They shared a long look. Lucas's eyes moved as he studied Ben's face, his eyelids lowering as he leaned closer and kissed Ben again.

They each kept one hand on me the entire time, Lucas's sliding to the side of my neck, Ben's on my waist. When they separated, both of them breathing heavily, they turned to me—first Ben, then Lucas—and kissed me just as deeply, our lips sliding wetly, tongues rubbing. Heat exploded inside me, bliss blazing through me from fingertips to toes.

Ben still wore a leather jacket, and he let go of both of us long enough to pull it off and toss it on a chair. Then we were kissing again, all of us, Ben's mouth on mine, then on Lucas's, and I watched with rising excitement and hunger.

It felt right. It felt perfect. It was the way it was supposed to be between us. All three of us loving each other.

I moved behind Lucas and let my two guys continue kissing. I hugged Lucas's waist, pressing my face to his shoulder, still watching them. Intensity heightened, their breathing growing faster, kisses getting harder. Ben nipped Lucas's chin. Lucas groaned. Ben touched Lucas's face, one hand sliding around the back of his neck, drawing him even closer, his other hand rubbing down Lucas's torso to find his erection. He caressed Lucas's cock through his jeans, rubbing his face against Lucas's.

He unbuttoned Lucas's shirt and shoved it off his shoulders

partway down his arms. Lucas started to reach behind him, but I was there to pull the shirt the rest of the way off. I slid my hands around him from behind, pressing myself against his naked back.

"Haylee." Lucas covered my hands with his. "Take your clothes off. Want your skin against mine."

I stripped the thick hoodie off over my head and hooked my thumbs into the loose yoga pants to drag them down my legs. My socks came off too, leaving me in panties and bra—a freakin' ugly sports bra that made me want to roll my eyes.

I moved closer to Lucas again. "One day, I'm going to wear something sexy and lacy when we have sex. Maybe even pink."

Both guys gave choked laughs. "Babe," Lucas said, "like you best naked when we have sex."

I smiled and settled my hands on the smooth, warm skin of his waist. His body quivered and tightened as Ben unfastened Lucas's jeans. When Ben drew his cock out and stroked it, Lucas let out a long, ragged groan. "Fuck that feels good. Goddamn."

"Yeah." Ben dipped his head to watch. "Fuck yeah. Wanted this so bad . . . your big stiff prick in my hand. In my mouth." He glanced up at Lucas almost shyly. "In my ass."

A hot thrill shimmered through me, and it was my turn to moan.

"Yeah," Lucas breathed.

"Want you to fuck me," Ben said.

Lucas reached for him and slid his hands down over Ben's ass. Lucas's muscles flexed as he gripped Ben. "Yeah." Then he released Ben and pushed his jeans and underwear lower on his hips, then all the way off. Lucas lifted his chin at Ben, who in response yanked his sweater over his head and took off his own jeans.

Lucas turned to me, wrapped me up in a breath-stealing squeeze, kissed me hard, then released me. "Babe. On the bed." I stepped away, but he stopped me with a finger in the back of my sports bra. "Wait. This needs to come off."

I peeled it off while I moved to the bed. I sat on the side and tugged my panties down and off, then climbed in. The covers were still rumpled and twisted from that morning. Ben and Lucas were both beautifully naked now, studying each other. My heart gave a warm squeeze at their expressions. Yeah, there was lust, but also awe and respect and wonder.

They joined me on the bed and for a moment we all sat looking at each other. Yes, it was just a tad awkward, for the first time ever. Then Lucas gave his sexy lopsided smile. "I have no idea what the fuck to do," he confessed.

The air lightened, and Ben and I smiled too.

"Maybe I should just watch," I offered.

Ben and Lucas frowned.

"I'll be right here."

They still looked doubtful.

"It's actually hot watching you two," I shared, peeking up at them through my eyelashes. "Really hot. I confess I might have fantasized a time or two about that."

"No shit," Ben murmured, reaching for Lucas.

"No shit," I confirmed solemnly, and once again I watched them kiss.

Then Ben drew back, and, touching Lucas's face, staring into his eyes, he said, "Whatever you want, Luc. Fast or slow . . . top or bottom. Just wanna make it good for you."

Lucas's eyes closed and opened in a slow blink. "Fuck," he muttered. "Not even sure what I want."

"Then let's just fool around and do what comes naturally." Ben smiled. "Let's fool around with Haylee."

I smiled at them as they moved, one on either side of me. This was fine. This was good. Fast or slow . . . however it happened . . . if it was me who brought them together, I was down with that. I was *thrilled* with that.

Lucas reached down and shook out the bed covers, drawing

them up over us, and we all slid down deeper into the bed. My guys took turns kissing me, long and sweet, lush and wet. And in between they kissed each other.

Their hands cupped my breasts, their heads dipped to take my nipples into their mouths in hungry draws. My head went back into the pillows, my fingers sliding through their hair as fire rippled beneath my skin. Sensation streamed to my pussy, which ached with need.

Having come so close to losing this, to losing both of them, gratitude and appreciation swelled inside me, adding an additional layer to everything I felt. There was also the profound relief and dazzling joy that Lucas and Ben had come to find each other. And me. And it was right.

In my head I knew how odd most people would find this, but my heart could only sing with happiness that we were together like this. Again, their heads were so close together, so close they could touch —and this time they did, looking at each other with seductive smiles before joining their mouths above me. Perfect.

They caressed my body from shoulder to hip, over my thighs, parting them and finding my center where I was wet.

"Babe." Lucas slid his fingers between my legs. "Are you that turned on?"

"You know I am. I always am with you guys."

They growled their appreciation.

But I was losing patience, my pussy aching with need, my entire body burning. "Would you two get on with it?"

They lifted their heads again, exchanged a wordless glance that now made perfect sense, then turned their eyes on me. Lucas's eyebrow went up along with the opposite corner of his mouth, and Ben grinned.

"Hmm. Someone's impatient," Lucas drawled.

"She's not the only one." Ben gave Lucas a pointed look.

"You said we could go slow." Lucas held Ben's gaze as he shifted away.

Ben groaned and reached for his hard cock.

Lucas lifted his chin, back to taking charge. "You get on Haylee and fuck her. I'm gonna fuck you. I'm gonna fuck you both."

Ben sucked in air at Lucas's blunt, bossy words. Color flooded his face. "Yeah," he whispered. I smiled and held my arms out. He moved over me, kneeling between my legs, nudging my thighs apart. His muscled shoulders and chest filled my vision, then he bent to give me a fast, hard kiss. "Love you, sweetheart."

"Love you too." Our eyes met in a sultry exchange.

I reached for a condom from the bedside table, hesitated, then pulled out two. I handed one to Ben and the other to Lucas, shivering at what that meant.

Lucas paused. He lifted an eyebrow at Ben. "Can I put this on you?"

Ben drew in a sharp breath, then his mouth tipped into a slow smile. "Yeah."

I watched with big eyes as they rolled condoms onto each other, the sight of their hands on each other's cocks erotic and beautiful. I melted even more, liquid heat drizzling down inside me.

Lucas looked up from Ben's cock where his fingers lingered. "There's a bottle of lube in that drawer too. Can you reach it for me, babe?"

I found it and handed it to him. Ben's lips parted and his breathing quickened.

"Fuck, this is nuts." Lucas reached for Ben's enormous cock with slick hands. "Ben . . ."

"Yeah. Right here. It's all good." His head fell back and he groaned, bottom lip caught between his teeth as Lucas stroked him.

"Can't believe this. Can't believe I'm doing this. Wanna fuck you so bad . . ."

My pussy clenched, and I hugged Ben's shoulders.

We'd done this before. It was beautiful. But now it had changed, with Lucas at Ben's back, pressing him down. Now it was so much more. Ben found my entrance, probed, and pushed inside me with that familiar, delicious stretching, that pressure, stroking over inner nerve endings. He eased himself in gradually, coming down over me, burying his face in the side of my neck. With one hand I reached for his hard thigh, my other hand clutching his back.

Lucas moved closer behind Ben, gripped his hips and rubbed against him. I watched Lucas's face, how it tightened into stark lines of erotic hunger. Ben shuddered against me, his hands going into my hair and tugging with sweet stings on my scalp. I petted his back reassuringly, murmuring soft words, and then Lucas pushed inside him.

"Tight, Jesus, fuck," Lucas muttered.

"'S'good." Ben's low groans were beautiful. "Yeah."

I felt it. I felt it physically—the additional weight, the pressure, the tensing of Ben's body against mine. I felt Ben's cock swell and pulse inside me. But I also felt it in my soul, such beauty and perfection and intimacy. The three of us joined like we'd never been before. Our bodies. Our souls. Our three hearts.

Who knew when we'd named our band that our three hearts would become one like this?

I cried out softly as they both began to move, mainly Lucas fucking Ben from behind, pushing him deeper inside me, over tender spots that flared to life, pleasure scraping over sensitive tissues. Fire spread through my body, coiling up tight inside me.

"Fuck, not gonna take long." Ben moved against me. "Inside your tight pussy, Haylee . . . and Luc in my ass. Christ, here it comes—"

"Fuck, me too." Lucas groaned. "Haylee . . .?"

"Close." I gasped, tilting my pelvis as much as I could beneath their weight. Ben rubbed against me—yes, right where I needed it—and I was so aroused and ready, it only took a few more drives of their bodies into and against mine to hurtle me up and over. Torn apart by the sensation that ripped through me, wild and hot and exquisite, I was unable to stop the cries that fell from my lips. I was sucked up into a shimmering, burning vortex, up and up, tossed over the edge to fall back down in a slow, pulsing drift.

Through a dark haze I heard their guttural cries, Ben's body shuddering and tensing against me, as they both came.

Lucas fell forward over Ben's back and found my mouth. Weight on his outstretched arms, he licked my bottom lip, then sucked it. Ben lifted his head and twisted his neck, and Lucas managed to kiss him too. Then Ben kissed me.

God. God. Unbelievable.

We collapsed into a damp tangle of sweaty limbs, heaving chests and pounding hearts. The guys shifted, someone may have gotten kneed in the nuts from the sound of a faint grunt, my hair got caught under Lucas's hand—it was messy and dirty and inelegant. And yet it was beautiful and brilliant, and everything I hadn't known I'd wanted. And I didn't want to lose it.

We cuddled. We played more. I watched Ben and Lucas stretch out on the bed on their sides in a sixty-nine position and suck each other off with slow, languorous mouths. The sheer beauty of their big wet cocks being held and licked and sucked, their mouths working each other, melted me to a pool of candle wax. Then they took turns eating me, this time not holding back from tasting me on each other's mouths, kissing each other in between licks of my pussy. Their lips and tongues spread heat through my body, giving me another astonishing, heart-quaking orgasm.

We slept for a while in a warm afterglow of languor and love. When I awoke, my guys stirring on either side of me, my gaze fell on the bedside clock. Twelve-oh-four. "It's Christmas."

"Merry Christmas, Haylee." Lucas kissed me, then Ben.

"Yeah. Merry Christmas." Ben rubbed my back. "Haylee . . . why don't you like Christmas?"

CHAPTER 13
WE'VE MOVED TOGETHER PAST YOU AND ME

Now we're one, as close as we can be.

Why didn't I like Christmas?

I sighed. "Lots of reasons."

Ben pulled me closer, and Lucas slid an arm around me from the other side. They already knew about my life as a kid, singing with my dad's band. But now I told them more, not just the facts but what it felt like—about the clothes I'd hated, how I'd had to work every night, how I'd just wanted to be a normal kid. "My mom died when I was seventeen." I had to halt a moment, my throat aching. "My dad was the one who had the band, made me sing. She'd gone along with it, because she wanted to make him happy, but at least she made it sort of bearable for me."

"Aw, Haylee," Ben murmured.

I swallowed. "My dad drank a lot. My mom tried to shield me from the worst of it. Tried to laugh it off, hide it, pretend everything was okay. I heard them arguing about it, when they thought I couldn't hear. After she died . . . there was nobody else there. Just him and me. He didn't care that I hated being dressed up like that and working on Christmas. He just drank more."

They both made sympathetic noises and stroked me.

"That year, after she died, we had a gig in a bar, a private party. Dad was sitting on a stool on stage playing the guitar, while I sang 'Holly Jolly Christmas.' I was smiling away even though it made my face hurt and I was dying inside, and . . . and then he fell off the stool. Right in the middle of the song. Everything kind of screeched to a halt. Just . . . silence. The guys in the band stopped playing, they were all just staring. I panicked, looking at my dad. My heart was pounding. I felt like I was going to throw up. And then the audience all started laughing." I took a breath, the memories burning inside me. "I just wanted to die. Or disappear. I wanted to run off the stage, but I had to get him up. He was so wasted he pulled me down too, in my stupid fancy dress, and we were both sprawled out on the stage. Probably my underwear was showing. He was laughing, like it was hilarious, and everyone else was laughing too. At me. Then people stopped laughing and started murmuring and whispering. Feeling sorry for me. I'd never been so humiliated."

"Haylee. Fuck."

"I got so mad at him that night. Once I managed to drag him off the stage, I was crying and screaming at him—why did he have to drink so much, how could he be so stupid?—I was mad at him . . . but I was mad at my mom too, for leaving me alone with him, for not being there." My voice got thick, and I had to stop and swallow a couple of times. "And Dad got mad too. He yelled back at me. He was a drunk, but he'd never yelled at me. I was shocked. Scared.

"And . . . I knew I was done. I had to wait until I graduated high school, but I was done. I was leaving. I decided I wasn't going to sing country music anymore." One corner of my mouth kicked up. "That didn't work out so well. But I also vowed I would never, *ever* perform Christmas songs again." My body had tightened despite their soothing touches. I took a breath and settled into their warm embrace, soaking in their love and letting it calm me. "Never. And I never did. Until last night."

"Babe." Lucas touched my hair, my face. "Why didn't you tell us? Why'd you do it?"

I swallowed, my throat thick. "I did it for us. For . . . you."

"Christ. We didn't have to do that."

"It was important for our careers. Brandon said so."

"Oh, honey," Ben murmured. "That's why you were so . . . uh . . . grouchy last night?"

"Yeah. I'm sorry."

"'S'okay, sweetheart. You did great."

"Yeah." They both chucked and I smiled. "I mean, *we* did great, and you know what? I actually enjoyed it. I *loved* it. Because . . . I was with you."

I felt the change in the air in the room, the way it went warm and charged.

"Babe," Lucas said. "Always. We're always with you."

My throat constricted and emotion vibrated inside me. I struggled for control of my voice. "I was sitting in front of the Grand Ole Opry today. Doing a lot of thinking. My dad dreamed of playing there. I knew he was never going to do that. But *my* dreams *have* come true. And I feel guilty about it. I have so much . . . especially now. I should go home. I want to see if he's okay."

"Haylee. Don't feel guilty."

"I can't help it." I grimaced. "I know I had to leave. I *had* to. But I wish he was proud of me instead of resentful."

"Maybe," Ben said slowly, "he wasn't resentful. Maybe he just didn't want to be alone. Your mom had just died. Sounds like that hit him hard. Then his daughter left too."

I closed my eyes. My throat burned. My chest ached. "Oh my god." Tears stung the edges of my eyes. "Now I feel even shittier."

"No, babe," Lucas said quietly. "You had to get out of there.

You couldn't have stayed there just because he didn't want you to go. You're not responsible for his drinking. It wasn't up to you to fix his life."

"I can't imagine that he's *not* proud of you," Ben added.

"If he can forgive me . . . and if he's still singing . . . maybe he could sing with us sometime." I bit my lip, glancing at Lucas on one side of me, then Ben on the other. "Just one song."

"That would be cool." Ben's eyes were warm. "Sweetheart, if you want to go see him and try to fix things between you, we'll come with you."

My heart filled up with love, squeezing the breath out of me. "Our relationship will be hard to explain." Which raised the bigger question. "It'll be hard to explain to anyone."

"We don't have to explain anything," Ben said. "This is our business."

I looked back and forth between them. "People are going to talk. You know they are."

"Let 'em."

Lucas frowned. "She's right. People will talk. We need to be prepared for that. We need to face the fact that we're never going to walk down the street, all three of us, holding hands or kissing in public. We need to face the fact that rumors are going to fly as time goes on and there aren't any other people in the picture . . . girl-friends, boyfriends, wives, a husband for Haylee. We need to talk about marriage and kids."

"Whoa!" I burst out. "Slow down, Lucas. I'm not ready for kids. Or marriage. Can't we just cross that bridge when we come to it?"

"You willing to give up the idea of marriage and kids forever?"

I swallowed. "Um. No." I thought about that for a moment. I obviously couldn't marry two guys, but I loved them both so much. The idea of having their babies . . . whoa. My insides clenched with both fear and wanting. "I know this is really weird. But we have the rest of our lives to figure it out."

"What about our careers?" Ben asked.

We all looked at each other. We all understood that there was a risk to our careers. A huge risk. I thought about it. I thought about losing it all. I thought about doing it without them. And I was the first to whisper my thoughts. "I can't imagine doing this without you guys."

Their eyes softened and warmed.

"I feel the same," Ben said.

"Me too." Lucas nodded.

If we made this choice, this unconventional choice, if we wanted this unconventional relationship, were there things we had to give up? Sacrifices to make? I didn't know the answers . . . but together we would figure them out.

"You guys are missing Christmas with your families."

Their eyes met, then turned to me. "We want to be with you, Haylee," Ben said. "You're our family."

"Yeah," Lucas agreed. "We'll call our folks tomorrow and explain things." I stared back at him, and he smiled. "Somehow."

"I would love a Christmas where we could just be home . . . together," I said. "Just us, doing whatever we want. Me in my sweats and drinking beer, with no makeup on. Nobody making us do anything. Nobody fighting. I hated it that you guys weren't getting along. It scared me."

"Sorry, hon." Ben touched my face.

"Do you really hate dressing up that much?" Lucas asked

I hitched a shoulder. "I'm used to it. I do it for you guys. Because I want us to be successful, and because . . . I love you."

"You don't need to do it for us." Ben frowned. "You wanna wear sweats on stage? Fine."

"Fuck yeah. Wear whatever the hell you want," Lucas added.

I smiled. "Thank you. But you know what? You guys believe in me. You give me the confidence to wear that stuff and not feel like a complete idiot, because you accept all of me. I used to feel like a fraud, wearing makeup like a mask and sexy clothes, like I was pretending to be someone I'm not. But . . . that last night on stage, in Sioux City—and the other night at the Ryman—I felt like I really was beautiful."

"You *are* beautiful." Ben nuzzled my ear. "Gonna tell you that over and over."

"Fuck, yeah." Lucas stroked some hair off my face.

"Thank you. That's what I mean. That means so much to me."

"You're beautiful, yeah, no makeup, whatever," Lucas said. "It doesn't matter what you wear. Although I have to admit some of those short skirts and low-cut tops and sexy shoes are pretty hot . . ."

I grinned.

"But even without those, you're beautiful," Ben said. "It's not just about what's on the outside. It doesn't matter what you wear. You're beautiful because you're *you* . . . talented and funny and caring. When I'm in one of my moods, you crack a joke and make me laugh and it's like the clouds open up and the sun shines."

"Yeah," Lucas agreed. "I know I get too serious and single-minded sometimes, and you lighten me up and make me realize it's not just about the goal—it's about having fun along the way. You love what you do so much, and you make me realize . . . I do too."

My throat swelled and ached, and I gazed back at both my guys with so much love and gratitude I couldn't even speak. I reached my arms out and hooked them both around their necks. "You guys. I love you."

They kissed me again, so sweetly, and then both whispered to me: "Merry Christmas, Haylee."

More Love
by
Haylee Tremayne, Lucas Doan, and Ben Radcliff

I shouldn't want these things,
    Especially from you.
    I've never felt this way before.
    Your touch, your smile, your arms around me
    Make me feel so beautiful.
    Waited all my life, wanted so much more
    Didn't know what I wanted was gonna be so hard
    And I don't want to lose this.

But you make me feel so beautiful,
    You make me feel so right.
    You make me burn and want to fly,
    You make me smile and make me sigh.
    You make me want things I've never had and fill me up with
wanting more—
    More love.

I'm lost, aching and longing for something I can't have.
    Pleasure like this makes people do crazy things.
    You make me lose my mind.
    Part of me wants to stop,
    Part of me wants to go,
    Part of me wants to know
    Because I don't know how to do this.

(He sings)
    Gonna show you how to do this,

Gonna show you how to fly.

Gonna make you smile and make you sigh.

Gonna make you want things you've never had and fill you up with wanting more—

More love.

It's all changing, there in our bed,

    Growing into something more

    Like a song moving from verse to chorus,

    Just don't know how the song's gonna end.

    Drowsy and drunk, feel like I'm floating,

    Can't stop myself from caring,

    Even though my heart still hurts.

But you make me feel so beautiful,

    You make me feel so right.

    You make me burn and want to fly,

    You make me smile and make me sigh.

    You make me want things I've never had and fill me up with wanting more—

    More love.

We kept our feelings locked deep inside,

    So deep we didn't even know them.

    Wanted you for so long, then I finally had you.

    We've moved together past you and me

    Now we're one, as close as we can be.

    Can't believe you love me too

    And it's not wrong because we should never be ashamed of love.

You make me feel so beautiful,

    You make me feel so right.

You make me burn and want to fly,

You make me smile and make me sigh.

You make me want things I've never had and fill me up with wanting more—

More love.

EPILOGUE

Two years later . . .
   Country Tunes Magazine *Christmas Edition*

After last month's Grammy win for Best Country Song with their smash hit "More Love," country music trio Three of Hearts has another reason to celebrate. Haylee Tremayne has confirmed she is pregnant with her first child. She is not, however, divulging who the father of her baby is.

   None of the three band members are married or in apparent relationships, and in fact all three share a home in Nashville. There has long been speculation on the nature of their relationship and whether Haylee is romantically involved with either of her bandmates, Lucas Doan or Ben Radcliff. The three musicians neither confirm nor deny any of these rumors.

   This reporter says, when they make music that beautiful, who cares about the nature of their relationship? All three are wildly popular with their fans and greatly respected by fellow musicians. They give much back to the community and they obviously care about each other. Like their song says—"never be ashamed of love." Congratulations on bringing more love into the world with the coming birth of a child, and Merry Christmas, Haylee!

OTHER BOOKS BY KELLY JAMIESON

Heller Brothers Hockey

Breakaway

Faceoff

One Man Advantage

Hat Trick

Offside

Power Series

Power Struggle

Power Play

Power Shift

Rule of Three Series

Rule of Three

Rhythm of Three

Reward of Three

San Amaro Singles

With Strings Attached

How to Love

Slammed

Windy City Kink

Sweet Obsession

All Messed Up

Playing Dirty

Brew Crew

Limited Time Offer

No Obligation Required

Aces Hockey

Major Misconduct

Off Limits

Icing

Top Shelf

Back Check

Slap Shot

Playing Hurt

Big Stick

Last Shot

Body Shot

Hot Shot

Long Shot

Bayard Hockey

Shut Out

Cross Check

Wynn Hockey

Play to Win

In it to Win It

***

Dancing in the Rain

Love Me

Friends with Benefits

Love Me More

2 Hot 2 Handle

Lost and Found

One Wicked Night

Sweet Deal

Hot Ride

Crazy Ever After

All I Want for Christmas

Sexpresso Night

Irish Sex Fairy

Conference Call

Rigger

You Really Got Me

How Sweet It Is

Three of Hearts

Loving Maddie from A to Z

ABOUT THE AUTHOR

Kelly Jamieson lives in Winnipeg, Canada, and is a best-selling author of over fifty romance novels and novellas, including her popular Rule of Three series. Her writing has been described as "emotionally complex," "sweet and satisfying," and "blisteringly sexy." She likes coffee (black), wine (mostly white), shoes (high heels), and of course watching hockey! She loves hearing from readers, so please visit her website at www.kellyjamieson.com or contact her at info@kellyjamieson.com.

Website: www.kellyjamieson.com
Goodreads: http://bit.ly/kellyjGR
Pinterest: www.pinterest.com/kellyjamieson

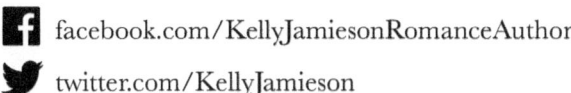

facebook.com/KellyJamiesonRomanceAuthor
twitter.com/KellyJamieson

EXCERPT FROM RULE OF THREE

Want more *ménage à trois* romance from Kelly Jamieson? Check out this hot excerpt from RULE OF THREE…

Chris's gaze drifted off to the side and she followed it. He was looking at those two girls, still dancing together, bodies now pressed together, back to front, the girl in back sliding her hands over the hips and stomach of the girl in front.

She glanced at Chris's face, went onto her tiptoes to speak into his ear. "I thought two girls didn't excite you."

He smiled. "It'd be hotter if one of them was you."

Her eyes flew open wide. "What!"

He grinned and pulled her closer.

"You want to watch me and another girl?" she asked incredulously.

His breath tickled her ear. "Watching you with anybody would be a turn-on."

Holy crap. How did she not know this about him? Kassidy pulled back to look into his eyes. "Really?"

The corners of his eyes crinkled but he held her gaze steadily. "Really."

Heat suffused her body. She didn't know what to say. Chris was so…straight. Did he expect her to make that kinky fantasy come true? Or was it just that—a fantasy?

The music changed and without saying a word, they left the dance floor and returned to their couch. She picked up her drink and downed the rest of it in three big heat-quenching gulps. Oh god.

"I'll get you another one." Chris flashed a knowing smile.

She sat there in a bit of a daze until the sofa dipped beside her. She turned quickly, thinking it was Chris back already with her drink, but it was Dag. His dark intent eyes fastened on her face. "How're you doing?"

"Good!" She gave him a bright smile. "You? Having fun?"

He shrugged, sipped his drink again—Scotch? Probably.

Chris returned with drinks. He couldn't sit beside Kassidy because Dag was there now, but she didn't want him to sit far away on another couch. Then Dag shifted away from her, pulling her with him so there was room for Chris on her other side. She took her drink from Chris, shoulder-to-shoulder with big, warm maleness on both sides of her.

Other friends came and sat too, and they all talked and laughed while Kassidy tried to ignore the achy fullness in her pelvis.

After a while, Dag said, "Come dance with me, Kassidy." He set down his drink and rose to his feet. He held out a hand, and she looked at Chris, who smiled and nodded. She took Dag's hand and followed him back to the dance floor, feeling a little like she were being led down a dark downtown alley at midnight, nerves fluttering in her tummy and her pulse leaping.

They moved to the music, a throbbing Latin drumbeat. Dag was a good dancer—of course—nothing flamboyant, but he knew how to move his body with an athletic grace. She let herself absorb the music, let it move her body, never taking her eyes off his face. When the rhythm slowed and merged into a slower song, he slid his hands over her waist, hips, around almost onto her ass. His heat enveloped her, the scent of his sultry aftershave filled her head as she slid her arms over his shoulders. Their hips moved together to the beat of the music.

Sex.

It felt like sex. Liquid heat slid through her body and pooled between her legs.

She bit her lip and looked over to where Chris sat. He'd crossed one ankle over the other knee, one arm stretched out along the back of the couch, looking so big and handsome and watching them.

Watching you with anyone would be a turn-on.

He lifted his chin in acknowledgement of Kassidy's glance. She was almost afraid to tear her gaze away from him and return it to the dangerous man she was dancing with.

"Chris is watching," Dag said.

"Yes."

"He likes to watch."

Dag knew that about him?

Their gazes locked. His hands slid lower on her hips, to just below the curve of her ass and his fingers moved. Dear god, he was pulling up her skirt. And it was short enough to begin with. Her pussy pulsed.

The silky fabric slid higher, bunching a little beneath Dag's fingers. "What are you doing?" she asked him through tight lips.

"Giving your boyfriend a show," he said with a wicked glint in his eye.

"And everyone else in the bar."

But she didn't stop him.

"Nobody else is paying any attention to us. They're all watching those girls."

The female couple was now dancing even dirtier, grinding their bodies together. They were so beautiful and sexy it was hard to take her eyes off them.

"Hot," Dag said. They watched. The girls turned to face each other again, and then they kissed. A long, lingering kiss on the mouth, hands buried in each other's long hair.

Dag and Kassidy looked at each other. The air sizzled around them. They were both aroused and maybe that was why she let him continue to ease the skirt of her dress up, his hands on her hips sliding the fabric higher. She looked back at Chris, now with both feet on the floor, leaning forward with elbows on his knees, still watching them, his gaze scorching her with erotic intensity.

And maybe that's why she still didn't stop Dag. She was pretty sure the cheeks of her butt were showing now—she was wearing a pair of cheeky panties, but they didn't cover much.

Then Chris was striding toward them, joining them on the dance floor. He pressed against her back, his erection hard against her, and nuzzled her neck. The three of them danced together, hard bodies pressed against her front and back.

Chris pulled her hair aside to mutter in her ear. "That was so fucking sexy." She pressed her ass back against him, tightened her fingers on Dag's shoulders.

"Your girlfriend is hot, Chris," Dag said.

"I know."

www.ingramcontent.com/pod-product-compliance
Lightning Source LLC
Chambersburg PA
CBHW050820180626
46814CB00004B/1391